Cursed book
The curses are endless

Dark Empire (Age Unknown)
Thunder from heaven with frenzied force, and rain pours in abundance, like a waterfall falling non-stop in this shitty weather. inside this palace the Sheikh took this guy who was jogging through the arcades

Falling on the stairs, breathing heavily and freezing, he carried in his hand a bottle with a transparent and transparent liquid of red color and made turns to the right and left, as if in a hurry, until he reached a large room.

They find on the walls of their shelves so many carrying bottles and powders and painted skulls and various things, for you do not know the priests in this dim light emanating from these torches, which leaves a dying flame for their long time

That give a shadow to this place like ghosts watching the room free of furniture and almost lost their hat a small table there in one of the corners a candle was arranged almost ended in silence

There was a strange smell in the office, similar to the smell of a grave in a dark corner, a simple bed settled down and you will hardly notice it at first glance he should have held them out to a gray-haired man and the owner of a long white beard.

She nestled on his chest and from his mind that time can eat her and not leave cuts on his face, but the hole has signs of old age.

A man who holds a bottle came up and said not in a whisper

- I understand everything, sir.

Grizzly saw a man in difficulty and said B and he slowly opens his eyes

-------- No need, (to barricade) you can't go anywhere, and medicine tells me about it.

Kneeling next to the bed and clutching his heart between his ribs like a small child, he said, almost crying:

-------------------- But, Your Honor-

The old man interrupted him, saying that he was giving up his fingers, which were stuck to the skin to the bone.

"Don't waste time, my son, and listen to me. I didn't have time for this, I see death calling me

He firmly said that he was afraid to part with the old woman, as tears receded from the barricade dear to his heart.

"Don't say that, sir.

The old man interrupted him and said again:

- That's right, the building and all the dead children are dead and we all return to earth

Warmly bending down with his head buried in the lapels, he raised the old man, put his hand on the old man's head and said in a trembling voice sad Beijing

- Don't cry and listen to me!

He raised his head and said in a choked voice:

- Yes, sir, I can hear you.

The old man smiled and spat in a very difficult statement

- You know that you only help the forum, and I am from the Lord, and you, and your daughter, before you help the forum, and that is why I will reveal to you a secret that you have not heard before

The old man is silent and swallows saliva with difficulty.

- This secret is what made the Queen remain without this last secret in her life.

The old man's silence made him swallow his saliva and speak the words of the weak.

- This secret lies in the book

A surprised voice interrupted him:
Book? -

- Yes, my grandfather and grandmother lived in the book, who collected it and their material, and generation after generation undertook to write a book that keeps between its pages the greatest secrets of past civilizations, how did they come about and how they collapsed and how they got lost in oblivion?

The old man's silence made him swallow saliva, and the shadow of a flame danced across his face like ghosts dancing to the melody of a hidden world.

- And I am the last one to finish the book, he finished it, but I thought before he had no hand, they greet me with face cream and not only bring company and I know very well that the queen does not want a book in a thread, but wants to rule the world through science and secrets and news of past civilizations

Shut up old man to score in your strength

"I often thought to destroy it, but I was afraid of the devastation of Queen B. I would return every time the builder has not finished yet, but now she cannot do anything to me.

Lester's silence is dominated by the most understandable (the barricade) to wrap up the front of a son who is afraid of his father.

! - Sir!

A fat old man didn't seem to hear him after I calmed down from a cough

- The book is here, under my head, take it and run away from this kingdom and destroy it. make sure he does whatever he wants, just don't let him go back to Leeds, and trust me son, Walch ... ------------ T

The old man's silence is always screaming (barricade) and he shakes his uncertified group hard by the master

- Sir !! -

He did not want this, he died after being removed from the shoulders of this great secret, and the other was crying in the heat, and he buries his face in the lapels of the master he had raised, but he suddenly remembered the conversation, at first he raised his head, thinking, he put hand on the pillow that lay on his master and the book, and saw admiration, and lowered his right and left hands until the sound of steps approaching him came to his ears, so he quickly tucked the book between the folds of his clothes, looked at the master and kissed him, then went to the window and opened it, before you jump take a last look at your master and said

"I promise, sir, that I will not fail you, no matter what, even if I pay with my life.

I took a roar from the sky and strongly shows lightning between that and then and there one of the corps entered and what he saw even exclaimed

- You !!!

Wasted (Shaft) time and quickly jumped to the ground and rolled, and then got up and took me, being amazingly fast and a schoolboy, calling for the rest of the war, as the owner has an emphasis in the dark, the story of the lady's body disappears and the matter is confused.

Did you manage to fulfill his mission?

And you?

* * *

These white birds flew in the sky and below was our friend (barricade) Running down the accelerator until he reached the ruins of this abandoned city

- He said to himself, panting from overstrain, from the effort in running.

"See what you'll do to the queen when you hear about the Ferrari of the royal palace with the book?"

He answered himself took the fear of the amount

"Of course they will look back at the book, even if the cost is the loss of my soul.

During his dialogue with himself, he had the curiosity to knock on the door of his mind and finish it bit by bit, curious if the Queen was forgotten.

this? See what this book has between the folds to the file to search for it madly

When this limit is killed by a monster, shit before that knows what he is doing to reach out to catch the book helps to open and during this I did not notice these thieves and they sneak around invisible as if they were a group of ferocious leopards pursuing prey from each side and at that moment pointed to them, their leader attacked nearby and made space with a loud cry coming out of his throat (barricade) Announcing his End, evil killed him, killed him and cut off his control and fell into the grass in silence and warm blood flowed abundantly from this body, laid on the ground and quietly cleansed by the leader of the robbers with blood-red blood from under his sharp blade, spoken in the roughness of his voice, that hoarse that attracts writers from under the fingers of a dead man who accepted waning with disgust.

Oh dirty books - what is this son of a bitch doing? -

- exclaimed another in dementia and, apparently, from his disdainful appearance, he suffers from the palaces of my mind.
- Give it to me, boss. maybe he runs out i

Laughed all the robbers said their leader sarcastically

- Where did you learn to be men, you idiot?

The latter laughed at the stupidity as happy as their leader reflected

- Probably, the graphics and colors are beautiful. I love her.

Like my boss twisted his mustache talked a lot

When you really are an idiot.

The latter laughed at this stupidity, laughing at the time when he said that his leader

- In that case, take out Fedya

Threw the book to the leader to the last length and lowers it between his hands and the rest of the thieves and reduces the body of the dead man (barricade), maybe they will find something useful to justify why they could find something valuable, and not the only book for its leader

It seems that this guy killed him there, and there is nothing to hold him back, except for this stupid book -

The chief's laugh speaks, his voice is hoarse, he rides his horse

- Dead New add to of killed them and welcome them in our history black

And everyone laughs as they ride horses, they go after their leader, and the one who has the book speaks quickly

I'll put it on (output) on the grid used in the afterword -

Following the thieves who left this place, passing also green fields and canals, until they arrived in the desert in the course of their fallen book, not noticing anyone in the sand, and they took a smiling book.

They seem to want ...

And it is produced in a fish liver and a book remained in the desert ... alone, as if watching the thieves and their disappearance, on the distant horizon, there was one thing left in the office, which is now located

Images

Yes, only sound and ----

Dogs

* * *

In the fish liver they take this Eagle prey, spin it into reason and from time to time believe that they are shouting high and declaring that the master of the sky and accepting the spins of the web for prey, his stomach has been empty since the morning and he has not tasted food, so that now suddenly his eyes flicker. there is something on the sand there may be a weasel or the rabbit the old man is dead, why waste time investigating he descended at lightning speed to get entangled between his fears and climb to the top in the meantime, he saw another eagle quickly attacking him, he could take on this is the prey of the Eagle first, and these are both distributed in the air and the fallen victims that were caught by the eagle first they were not the prey of the book of the damned who fell at the speed of a stone Descending from a height to identity in the nozzle of a tall mountain in the middle of the desert and tumbling down so quickly, so settles on a smooth rock at the foot of this mountain and scatters dust around itself and everything else, even the dust is interrupted at a slow pace, but there is something strange there - as if a voice roars in Genappa this place, as if it comes from a creature that lies in the darkness of this mountain well, the light falling from the nozzle in front does not illuminate this place very well and ---------

Suddenly a hand reached out to a claw with a dark green trace, reminiscent of the scales of snakes, lizards, and took the book of the damned, and I led him to where, in the darkness and silence of all history, I saw a terrible question.

- Who is the owner of this terrible hand?

The answer was frightening to the extreme

Yes, scary to the limit

* * *

The next Old Time Unlimited

It was the full moon was a mediator between the stars, as if talking to them and telling them that I am the most beautiful day of you and more splendor today is Christmas here I look at the streets of Cairo the darkness was the streets are empty from passers-by and the lights are almost only some dim lights are coming out from the windows of this ancient house, no sounds, no sound of the worlds, the hungry wolf knows from time to time that he exists and that he longs to taste the warm blood and the words of the streets proclaim him a night watchman for the street and are vigilant and accept them as if they were in an endless war with me and all this rolls into the atmosphere of a peculiar smell imposed by women, at night and far away on one of the streets a ghost of something that is happening slowly and surely appears, as if he knows everything. Nice path in silence, stopping in front of one of the houses and then raised his stick and knocked on the door, and after a few seconds of waiting the door opened and very little of that flickering flag of light came out to show the features of a stranger that looked different from the source and it looks like he was in his forties or more, look at this server and he said he didn't expect a clear answer.

- Your master of the house?

The waiter smiled and gave a light smile among the white, like his clothes, a color contrasting with the color of his black and bald head and said in a very literary way, he whispered

- Will you tell me, sir?

- Tell him that I'm funny, I came to him on an important matter

The fact that I heard the server, which even crawled out because of a stranger who entered and looked back and forth, thought closer with white eyes, look, this is the first time he pored over an Arab house and walked on the spot, as stealthily, as snake, and suddenly heard the voice of the server, which says no

- Sir is waiting for you.

He walked in a circle in front of a strange house on two floors through two corridors in a few steps, then he stood in front of the door of one of the rooms and hit the door with a ring, and then the income is considered exotic, climbed to the roof of the hut and found that it was high, and found books and etc. On their walls, as in a huge library, and noted the presence of a simple office, put several candles in a small model of the globe and several books, and when he found a strange one sitting in this place, they said something, but he heard a voice coming from one of the staff said:

Welcome to my home, humble stranger.

Look, a strange source of sound, he saw a man of about seventy completely ruined his head and watched her mustache and chin shortly put on a simple cart with a smile in that sweetness that the bride always smiles when we approach any guest ..... The stranger's thing pointed to server come here the stranger exclaimed when they shook hands with the thing that is visible in his eyes.

- Sheikh (Abdullah) I was very tired until you arrived.

Disarming thing his palm from the palm of a stranger said it is a system check

- Perhaps the motivation is good, so please, - ------------

His right weird speed

- The Messenger of Allah (s) declared (Ay)

Silence (Jafar) and his hand, and his bit back, and took the checkbook, and took the supplements

- Actually, I've been looking for you for a long time.

- Looks like I'm an important person when they were looking for me a long time ago

Look at him strangely in speed without even including a semi-artificial smile, and he says

-You can't even imagine how important you are to me, my next life is available to you.
Laughter thing

"Is that why I'm so important?

Here, an allogeneic obsessed with a thing, is curious and decided to find out why he came, fear disappeared from his smile and features of novelty appeared in its place

- absolutely

- Let me come up to say hello and find out why you came

Taking (A.J.) crosses one of the books and pages into the ford strangely, as if he doesn't care, Yum-Yum or like a place, and speaks in a calm wonderful voice:

(Book of the Damned) -

You noticed all the facets of the thing and felt that there was lightning, you may be ready to start up as if you did not hear it

- What?

He did not leave the book (Jafar), but kept fiddling with it and said strange things to Brod

"Don't worry, senior me, and make it so that it remains a secret between us forever. if you give me half of the card that you have and I would like to calm you down and tell you that I know everything about you from the very beginning, that you have half the card and your passion, which has no boundaries for the dying Empire, and we also know that you have half a card .--------------

With every word spoken, fear grew in front of them, snapped back saying that he had taken fear of the amount

- Who are you really?

He answered simply:

- I am the one who came to you very far, I will take half of the card from you at cost price

There he was told directly and clearly, like a challenge

- They say I'll give it to you first?

What I heard (Ja'far), this phrase even threw the book out of his hand and turned around as if it wanted to hit him. the touch of madness was gone his eyes widened in a strange way, holding on to his forehead there was no creation of him in the form of a terrible, he says

---------- Give them to me, whether you like it or not, old man, what-

- Please, it does not need to hear me, the words hurt me and prefer to leave my house and make me get a favor to tell you the addict over yours.

In the challenge, as he approached in terms of what can be seen in his eyes (AJ) said

- I will not leave until I take what I came for. I've been looking for years

I feel like a thing, insisting on the words of the Messenger of Allah (s), without thinking to pull the rope, hung from the ceiling and was only a few seconds, so all the servants looked at them out of the corner of their eyes. he had the specter of a mocking smile that indicated that he had changed his mind.

"Do you think this will prevent me from taking what I want?"

Silence was said to see the degree of impact of his speech in the sight of things, and then follow the accent like the groan of a snake

- I would gladly tell you that you are a heel, this
Twice within a few seconds a said something to one employee:

- (Bile) get this egg out of the guest spam

What approach (Gallus) from (already) even went from his fist with lightning speed to settle in the stomach and leave all your service to flow freely, but he did something unexpected and completely contrary to all laws, and he grabbed his stick, to use it as a fulcrum, and began kicking the faces in circular motions so that they would fall quickly from the intensity of the blows, jumping with lightning speed like a clown to calm down behind (Galla), who are people freeing his eye in a strange way, and he lowered his lower jaw in horror when he saw that the Messenger of Allah (s) presses a stick on him, this speaks of a sharp blade to control the air, let's say in a geisler clearly:

"I'm not afraid to do anything to get what I came for, even if it costs me to walk over the bodies of everyone here.

Stop thinking about it at the moment, but this is more complete defiance and irritation to the limit.

- It's a good idea, old man, you don't have to do anything that you will regret later:

Here he saw a thing of seriousness and determination and in the eyes of the Messenger of Allah (s) and thinking about the fate of the service and their families after the minutes that seemed like hours, the Sheikh said:

- Well, Call (bile), and I'll give you what you came for.

Then the Sheikh opened a model of an earth globe and took out a roll of paper received by the Messenger of Allah (OV) and then laid it out on the desktop and pulled out the roll again, he folded his clothes and how good it was, the card was one in two unevenly for some reason and took it the owner smiles has his eyes, and then Tony and grabbed his stick said, Before leaving there is a big smile on his face, like a demon's smile is great:

- Thank you for being there .-----

Silence as he looked me in the eye a thing, and then follow:

- Old man

Taking Esther's laughter and accepting the sound of his laugh in Demon Street, we follow him from behind the glass of the window before smiling at the mist - the true elder runs into his office to recount it on paper and then folds them into his clothes and slides the last to swallow the fog in silence and far knows the consequences of the memory of the hungry wolf.

Photographing the leaves d

Determined that it stops

* * *

Inside this modest house, a meeting with our sheikh in front of this handsome boyish face, the owner of this heavy hair that grows on the forehead of his balloon, his body, his skin, his honey-colored eyes or two, and his body takes its sport:

- (Burgundy), my children will not believe what happened to me today !!

He swallowed this thing with his saliva, and a girl with a beautiful face entered with a light face, similar to the presence of angels in her purity and softness, and her eyes are blue, and her body, which supports the body of Venus, the goddess of beauty for the Greeks, according to the beauty of this dress Arabian turquoise and her black hair that looked like a starless night had reached the middle of her back, she carried teacups set side by side and listened to the thing she complements .:

- As you know, today and the future are connected with the past.

And they all love to tell you that there is a book that keeps all the evil between the folds, and that's why I came to you today and said ----

He (Tang) said emphatically:

- Who wrote this book?

The girl exclaimed asking this to another:

- Yes, uncle, we want to know where he got this book from?

Wait the creature said:

- Yes, (addressing Lily) I will tell you what is the link to information about the origin of the book

Silence to swallow your saliva, and then follow the voice of the entity as an excuse for conscience, bringing events to fiction for anyone who listens and speaks:

* * *

For millions of years there was a large kingdom ruled by a just king and a good wife this file with twins once had a child so beautiful and after many years the king died and she died his wife behind him was the sadness of the kingdom after the period of the Ascension of the king's son to the throne chair that angered his sister and his groups and after a long struggle divided the kingdom into two halves and a file with the name of the light Kingdom, and a file with the name of the dark Kingdom, but she did not forget the day when the other half of the kingdom became free on all paths and paths. it means, legal or otherwise, but witchcraft and black magic, a way to get his second half, and the years passed, an old man came, he leaves the door of her life, but she stops at nothing. And took the impulses and her witches with him. looking to be interested, to deceive the magic spell of black magic, to transfer her spirit into the body of another woman thanks to magic and demons succeeded and took moves from body to body. then, one day, someone told her a spell that there is science more than magic, if you knew it and worked, they could control the world. Here the King of Evil tried again and asked about it, they said that it was buried in Egypt, Babylon, they want every great civilization to end quickly and bring all the witches and scientists and their compilation of all these sciences and that they allow them as soon as possible and tell her that she can use these sciences to make a car fly in the sky. And dived into the water again and took the dream

And drive a miracle around the world with science to do its magic here and scientists have passed years, and everyone is working to ensure that we even finish the book One of the witches who awakened her conscience, suddenly decided to deprive the king, than strive for it and the book of the damned has already fled to Egypt and disappeared and shows no signs of the king's cheek and survives the book like a myth dreamed of by everyone in every place and closed the file, but I tried to find it everywhere, but her magic could not reach him and studied black magic for the book,

but she failed here, she cast a curse on the book, If you budge there
will be a face of it then

Elsewhere, I heard from one of the witches about the book and
heard about the Grand Prize that the Queen gives to those who live
in it. he took the amulet and tried to find out where the book was
and spent days and nights and months in hiding until he came out
with a map on it before he went to the queen to give her a card he
changed his mind and decided to go to his own and arrived at the
Egyptian desert with his daughter and only helped him, suddenly
this magician died and his daughter returned and forgot about the
book; the body of her father's wealth lay on the way of her return
and sorrow covering her to find someone lying in the desert,
between life and death escaped from tents and even recovered
their strength and invited him. he is the owner of the caravan
business captured the bandits and broke all knee He is the only
survivor of the convoy and quietly made his way into her heart with
his love and carved his story with it and learned some kind of
money magic and did not know that he was destroying his evil
mouth, I knew about the card, so he decided to rob her in a dream,
but she absorbed half of it and tried to pull it out, but he was the
strongest of them, he tried to stab her with a knife and blood from
her belly and did not believe that she loved and saved Lazebnik
tries to kill her and split the card in two halves and launched a spell
in front of him and tried to kill her, it was possible to find her by all
means, but she failed and was never found. this is what I tell him,
but one of the travelers who takes the bank found her, she has too
much blood, so he tried to tease her a week ago and she felt safe
with him, he told him the story she gave him Half cards must be
destroyed. without her, one cannot rise to the place that the book
of the damned and did so she turned her soul into that part, leaving
behind an unbearable task and the future no one knows except
God alone
- What story is hard to believe

She shouted (Lily) not to interrupt his story, and then asked her brother (Tanya) to say:

- And what will happen if someone finds this book of the damned?

Exclaimed without thinking, opened his eyes wide and raised his eyebrows

- My T / C, If you sign this book, the worst use will be in the hands of evil, there will be corruption and injustice in the world, instead the two kingdoms will look around him hungrily and will not be used by the Queen of Darkness until you get her at all costs , will spread throughout the world, will ultimately be unsatisfactory for everyone and will be the end of humanity.

The silence of the creature and what I saw is that my eyes (burgundy), which I took thinking about this source of a terrible state, disappointed him, seeing a terrible scene all the fire and smoke and debris and ruins and bodies in each place, he painted the maximum traces of horror on his face

- What a Sphinx, what a terrible fate

Follow the thing with his voice. essential

"In reality there will be more destruction than you can imagine, son.

- She exclaimed (Lily). :

- There must be some solution, uncle !!

- Yes, my child, there is a solution, and not ... - get the book before everyone else and name it

He was interrupted: (Tang) said:

- How is it, uncle, and your card was stolen?

- Yes, they stole from me, I know.

Buddy (Tan) is surprised to be asked:

- Are you touching us, uncle?

- Who said that, (Burgundy) I'll explain everything to you.

Silently swallowed saliva and watched this passion with his own eyes, and then followed it. :

- I stole this alien half of the map from myself, but you know it by heart so that I could send it and when the individual of the other half who was in the possession looked at it well and went to the bastard of my house, so I quickly drew it, and I came here, and here is the shore of the other half.

A separate thing, the paper was in his possession and the paper was different and stepped on them with valleys and mountains, signs and symbols, and then took beer and the next two in attention even when it came to the Red mark on one of the mountains

"Here, at the foot of this mountain, lies the book of the damned.

She is impressed by her uncle: (addressing Lily) exclaimed:

- What kind of person has a taste for wit, that it is best to go after the book yourself, and then destroy it, and we thereby saved the world from this danger.

He examined the (burgundy) lamp flame dancing on his face and spoke with calm stoicism:

- Risk of flight and you won't come with us.

She (Lily) that her brother wants her to leave, she stubbornly said:

"But I want to go with you, and I'll go.

Hub (Burgundy) from his place he turns the biggest of those who fear Him:

- Don't go.

The other, endowed with reality, and folding her arms across her chest, said decisively more:

- I'm leaving.

- Do not

- I'm leaving.

- Dude. Where (Burgundy) when I insist and many others

- I said no, it means no, and this decision is final, and there will be no discussion

(Lily's) her brother's gaze found strength and endurance somewhere in my eyes, so I decided to quickly leave my position and remained clean when s passed by, suddenly without warning she rushed from her place, and I rushed to the second floor and in heat anger ran up the stairs, and she was already thinking what to do to go with them, like her brother, so watch her until she disappeared, then what he said drew her attention:

- Everything I said about the book made them bring him to them, so that the thief would repent of his own, so as not to fall into the hands of a non-secretary

Then he added with great enthusiasm:

Isn't that right, uncle?

- exclaimed the creature. :

- Yes, T / C

(Tan) asked him quickly:

- So when are we going, uncle?

- Said the standing hub, his voice was deep .:

- If our meeting at dawn with the first strands does not take place

The fact that the talking thing finished the view of the roof of the house and did not notice (Lily) and she can fish, as if they intend for something (Lily) and turn to the open ceiling, which shows the Moon among the stars, as if watching what is happening in silence, wonderfully it seemed to everyone that he was smiling the sweetness of this was a charming sight that night, thus taking all the anticipation of dawn, so anxious to begin his journey in search of a book
The first strands of dawn, and the bird's command talk all around heralds the beginning of a new day, and far beyond the trees

The palm took the disk of the Sun, dyed it with a blood-red mixed orange dark sneaks silently, as if afraid to go out, down there, palm trees that were reaching for the sky - Sheikh (Abdullah) rose to unravel the structure of color, and the women matched the strands of his white hair, behind him silently while he looked at the road between the trees, as if he were waiting for someone to appear, and behind him stood his gray horse, walking along the path completely different and it was only seconds until I sat down his ears forward to catch a very free thing for us that says:

- And what is there, my friend? .- You see something that I do not see!

And I almost finished my dialogue with the horse until a ghostly knight of the end of the Earth, a robber passing through a horse, comes up very quickly and I kill one more thing, so he smiled and said to himself:

- Finally, I came, I had a suspicion that you would not come!

Stop the rider before the creature falls from the horse, fiery red fluff reveals his face appeared and his features exclaimed the creature:

- Why are you taking so long?

The answer (Burgundy), which is breathless, the words come out choppy:

- She is my uncle's sister wants to come with us and insists on it.

Lift this thing so that she can see him off, his eyes shouted, his facial features are serene:

- And what did you do with her?

- Lie to her and tell her to go after her things, and if you come after me, then hurry up, I am God here, and let her hit on these matters again.

Here the facial features of the thing that were usually addressed to his biography were calmed down:

- No need to spend more time, and the costs of publishing in a lower light.

The leaders of my two horses of them, and leaves them together in this way, perhaps among the palms, until he disappeared from sight and never noticed this knight, who bends his white clothes, hides his face with a concentrated response to black, he watches them with his eyes from behind the high hill gives not a wide range of vision, and stood silently wondrous and the women played grab hold of his clothes, like a mythical scene and pinch the sun continues to rise unremittingly

Yes it stopped

* * *

Taking two going joints between the mountains and tall trees, intertwining branches, penetrating into the valleys between the tall grass of the savanna, and now the birds of the egrets fly in the sky, fearing them to break into his solitude, and pass like days, and the sun covers them, and both stand while the one and the other reached the pool filled with water, from the very last West on the beach birds sprout around flowers of different shapes and colors, the golden rays of the sun reflect on it, which gave it a charming look, and descend in tranquility from the horse, and leave it to eat. the grass, but he tended the water, and it between your palms and your tattoo could have been poisoned, so he knew about his outdoor life and found that Pei and he drank until the rose, and then filled closer, that he carried and washed his face and beard were white and then looked at (the wine) and told him that he shared his integrity:

- The earth is fresh, sonny, and it tastes very sweet

What I heard that I even landed quickly on my horse and knelt on the pond and even Roy is good and filled closer than others, I stretched out on my back and took to watch the heart of the clear sky, and took after the flocks of birds flying back and forth , and said::

- RO tell me more about the two kingdoms, I would like to know more

The hat thing at the edge of the pond looked at the page and said net, his voice thundered like Looking back into the abyss of time

- I will tell you about the kingdom of darkness.

Silence is a thing to swallow saliva or remember that it was news about this kingdom and complete it is still visible on the page that interest is slow

- This is the worst Kingdom that you know or have heard of a king who rules them with a whip and a collar of iron, not soft and not ruthless with hair and anything that has a straight and

Cutter (Burgundy) yells:

- And where to choose this kingdom and the whole world, which I had never heard before and which had never been before me one fine day, fell out of sight?

- The truth is that it never disappeared, but it is present in some place, no one knows exactly where this kingdom is, but for the record, the book of the damned is a fork in this kingdom of animals, and without them they are weak and do not show sound between the kingdoms that are around
- What a strange kingdom

"The strangest thing is that their queen put a curse on this damned book.

- What is the power of this curse?

- If you move the book from its place at the moment there will be a place, then to him with all my means and whatever it costs her the command to restore it at any cost, never retreat down the inner side of her finger, like a beast Crouching that spreads the signal around her mercilessly

- Is it such cruelty?

"But even more so that I have heard much less about it than I can tell you right now.

- Believe it, uncle, that the kingdom is ruled by a cruel woman, and the book is the science and civilization of the Ancient?

- No one will believe her son, but this is the only truth that I know now, try to accept them as they are, and do not reject them, mind you

The silent creature swallowed its saliva and immediately added

- No need to talk about it anymore and let's hurry up, he steals our

Which is almost a thing to finish him to the hub of reality and ride his horse as well as you (Burgundy), continuing to push his way until he disappeared beyond the horizon and never noticed this masked white knight who took over them close in a wondrous silence, like a predator tiger waiting to be attacked

Yes, the hours of the attack .... Next

* * *

Complete your journey to the middle of the desert together with great difficulty, especially in this sandstorm that took the buy little by little, I took the grains of sand slaps on their faces mercilessly, and the story of pain is still here and there he said (Burgundian) in difficulty that belongs to point one from the mountains raised one of his hands in front of his face, maybe he can prevent the collision of grains of sand biting him:

- Uncle, it seems we cannot continue our way to the center of this storm, it seems that it will not stop now, let's celebrate the blessing that there may be a refuge where we can until it calms down and calms down.

He heard how the creature in the difficulty of the wind took a whistle in its ears and said loudly:

"You're right, and let your vision harden, the sand scattering everywhere.

Cut two of their way to the front in extremely difficult even to get to it, and fortunately they found a cave. what is so educational in taking out what has stuck to them from the soft sand, and then sitting down and talking (burgundy) is accessible to the stage from its place:

- What a terrible storm!

- How's the desert, son.

Turned to (guilt), trying to steer the conversation back on track:

- He spoke to me about the kingdom of darkness, tell us if her sister is the kingdom of light.

Try to touch this thing to my back on the cave wall said:

- Ah, the kingdom of light.

Silence, as if he was trying to remember something, then he said, his voice thundered, he noticed passion in my (burgundy) eyes, like a small child listening to a fairy tale before bedtime.

- All that I have heard about her, as about some great kingdom, about huge palaces and high towers, about great clouds and waterfalls, about high lakes, wonderful, animals, so many of all shapes and colors, and variegated, and report about the water was filled with brilliant fish, and about her agriculture and industry, they are peaceful and do not like war, and about horses, and about all her employees, about all her families.
Burgundy, and he quickly asks, interrupting the conversation:

"And his ruler, like the Queen of Darkness, moving among bodies, is different.

- Not all of what I heard that their elder king died, others came and all descended from the same beautiful, and people bless them with this love, over the generations in this kingdom they are essentially a fairy tale about the book of the damned, which the Queen of Darkness committed, and they know how dangerous he is to the world. and here is to me all their ruler, that the book had time in its reign before you got the queen of darkness, this creates the story of their life.

"Have you ever visited your uncle in this kingdom?

- Never, but there must give us their news and what he saw there.

Silence, and he turned to exit, and then said:

It seems that the storm has stopped, we have lost the sun, the sun has reappeared, and the sand is us, my son on our way, the road ahead is long, and on the way I will tell you everything I would like to know.

Smile (burgundy) and Monday Javadi ran to meet them, walking in the very heart of the deserted desert, without water, and laying it out behind one of the sandy hills, a knight in a mask stood, pursuing them in silence, wondrous and terrible

* * *

Unless the disk of the Sun took me and took both birds back to their nests and took the night crawling slowly and losing the veil of black over everything, it is far away and flickering with light the last person returned (Burgundy) and they arrived at the ruins of this abandoned city, and I arrived before long as the sun with its light and when it landed a thing on its horse and help son, and took the thing to examine these ruins, said after a period of meditation in which I was:

"We will stay here for the night, you will not find a better place among these ruins.

The look (burgundy) around him was like a system of simple suffocation, blocking out the darkness in order to see what was behind the destroyed walls, and Sayid raised his eyebrows in surprise:

- Do you see why the owners went to these ruins?

He lifted this thing over his shoulder and said, looking at the ruins of this abandoned city:

- Boy, there are many answers when we know that we can, if one day we don't recognize her or even ask about her. he wanted my drink to say something, but what he says in no uncertain terms is sitting next to one of the walls

- Hmm, I have some firewood before the fire.

That is, just a few seconds, until I collect firewood and light a fire, and he was already sitting in front of his uncle to ask him if he danced facing the fire:

- What if we could and brought this book, Uncle of the Queen of Darkness, before this (ja'far) happens?

Answered Thing Worshiped With A Stick In The Gym Included Sheet

If we assume that we have completed ..

Cutter (Burgundy) that Grant stood on as if there was something there to get his attention.

- Wait!

I feel that there is no movement or sound coming from behind one of the walls called a company that walks quickly and calmly through hand-held photographs, and that the one who approached jumped up so quickly to see the owner of the photo, and when he saw him, he named his place and his eyes widened, and took a thing called worry.

- What is there, my son behind the wall?

The absence of his thought that something terrible had happened to him did not respond, and he got up and grabbed his stick and took the firing squad to the wall in silence and took the seconds pass like eons long and boring and the heartbeat quickens, and there are thousands of possessed and obsessed with racing and out-of-control plays, it will stop, but will it stop at all?
In this cave, this creature of an unknown author of a green fringe moves, which languishes between the one and the other, and his breath, bad breath awaits in the office, great and high humidity, and that light dim light falling from a nozzle high in the upper part of the cave one grabbed a box with a wooden decorative beautiful decorative graphics, and in a calm I tried this creature, which puts a patterned fund next to a black book on this gray rock, but did not realize that I could not fit them together, experienced the latter and fell to the ground, spread dust and opened the book wide, and Discussion and photographs of the colorful and amazing are observed by the creature when you take the oil falling from your mouth to the ground and grab the book between your palms. I would like to see or understand what is, and this is just seconds from meditation, even immersion in complete darkness and a perplexing question.

- Do you understand how important this book is?
The sky was dull in color, the solar disk disappeared like stolen, and bends away, despite the fact that the hours of the approaching night had not yet come, he was there, in space, dense clouds process him gloomily, send him to the psychology of fear, yet this is terrible , I took a large group of birds of crows flying away and for the second time as if they did not care about this terrible weather, and then I rose above these towers gray took a question, the

sounds are annoying, every now and then they endow this place with horror cleared of serious depression.

But it seems to the inhabitants of these towers that they do not care about them, do not vote, as before, and when we approach the window of one of the towers, we see that there is movement in it, it seems that she suspiciously took one of them, very quickly she climbs the stairs, then goes to the arcades, suffocates until it reaches the hall, its ceiling is very high, as if piercing the sky, and at the end of this round room with glass windows and giant hats, a throne of an enormous size of rock seems to have an applique in the form of a giant snakes, scary, and a sitting woman covered her head with a handkerchief, added a little to her face, it includes his features with these shadows that fell on her, and includes not only a small mouth, that nose of the rectum, sharp, with this cut My alabaster is relatively long, this leg is a large body, appeared in a garment of strange olive-colored features another dark one and shows the palm of her lily-shaped scepter glass is hidden among thorns a man took ATD quickly approaching, it is at the receiving end of his breathing with difficulty, then bent over quickly and quickly to cheer:
- Ma'am, when you give the latest news.

I haven't opened the file of her mouth yet, but the man heard her say in his head:

- This is what you have, soldier .. and I love to hear what I want to hear otherwise ----

The man smiled with his saliva in difficulty and, perhaps, felt himself dry from the blow of the queen's words, and after she was the same, he continued, as he wants to split the Earth from her eyes:

"I move animals frozen since ancient times, ma'am.

What I heard, saying this so gifted standing, and exclaimed, This time through her mouth, and her voice was harsh like a thunderbolt:

- When to move on?

"Now, madam, everyone is awaiting orders, Milord.

I never saw a man looking at her, she hid under this veil, but said:

- Go. I'll follow you right now.

A man ran quickly, and after a few seconds disappeared in front of her, and in the silence of the snakes she stood, as if lost in thought, and he did not ask her to be silent, raised her scepter to the sky of the mainland, told her, smiling in tons, even becoming close to the smile of a demon, came from hell .:

- Come, write dear and from there more, I know where you are, and I will come to you at any cost.

She raised her scepter ... until Pat seems to be under the ceiling of the hall and shouts over:

- Whatever the price.

Thunder in the sky roared powerfully.

* * *

Difficult seconds pass on our sheikh, who waits (for Burgundian) that his long absence behind this wall will blow him away, and after that he eats apples, a clever thing, shows his master next to his dog a familiar back pain; and if his legs were broken, call this thing, after the hiss of alarm has disappeared from his face:

- What is it, son?

Smiling at this sweetness, he looked at the floor:

- This is my new friend .. you see, my uncle broke his free leg and will not leave him here alone, I will have to make his leg a problem for us on our journey.

- Sonny stumbled, the best stuck to him and her.

I saw a dog wagging its tail, one of her eyes begging him quietly not to leave them.

But the joy is in his voice. parental:

- Do not think, son, leave it, it's good, believe me.

Around the fire sat (Burgundy) next to his dog, took the owner with a broken leg and took the creature that was pursuing them in silence, the light of the fire danced on their faces, and the moon rose in the sky, as if it was looking at them in wondrous silence.

Meanwhile, the creature exclaimed:

- We will stay here overnight, and tomorrow we will go.

Be quiet for a while and then walk calmly:

"We will be our journey without a word, broken.

I did not know (camp) and health and leave everything for tomorrow.

* * *

Taking this knight, accompanied through a horse through these cobbled streets by a rock rising near the sound of a horse's hooves in monotony, and bowing from one street to another in this city with white houses and high towers and huge gardens, singing waterfalls, the high water of which gives this place a scene from mythology, and that only seconds to stop in front of the Palace are mined by brown walls, tall towers, contains a hill high, then landed on his horse and began to climb the stairs up to the portico, then down to the vestibule of a giant full circle with large windows and high , and occupying large sections of the wall in a ring, it was decorated with drawings of an exquisite dwelling, which increased the place of beauty, and opposite the entrance sat the throne of a large and majestic king. There was a handsome young man with heavy black features that remained behind him, which increased his beauty, especially in such a strong wind, my eyes were set, his color was burgundy, and next to him was an older old man, he had green hair , a chin in white and black, as well as his hair, which rose from much of the introduction to his head, so that the floor was flawless, and he gripped with his hands a large stick formed by her head-shaped head of a ram with horns, a knight's bow in front of them in calmness, he spoke and his breathing received intensity from his efforts:
- Lord, king of the kingdom of light.

He nodded to the young king, smiling sweetly, lifted the knight's head and quickly exclaimed:

"We received a message from our spy in the kingdom of darkness.

The sweet smile faded, Walter was replaced by other profiles, the young king exclaimed:

- What is the meaning of this message?

- They say that the animals are moving and that there was an unusual movement in the file, as they do everything that surrounds it with full.

The King interrupted him, saying:

It is not yet known what kind of normal gas it is?

The knight said to Pratap and shook his head:

- Never, sir; they transmit it confidentially.

Taking the king, he thinks quickly, and in his head a million thoughts are mixed together, but he indicated to the knight to leave, and our place is fast, and the old man noticed that, even bowing to the king, he said in a low voice:

- It seems, sir, something happened that we feared.!

The king said the shard of sight:

- Until now, I didn't know for sure.

- Sir ... while you are moving the locked animals, the curse that put her file on the book must have been achieved, she moved the book, and it was known that her charm is where her level is and will gather sooner or later get it and register it in your favor.

- The king exclaimed and thinks that his eyes widened in the minister's words when he imagined the fate of people and that the queen rules everyone with the help of the science of the book, and with the help of her black magic, and with the help of the eyes of imagination, she saw a terrible fate for everyone.

- When you're right, Minister.

Yes, what have you ordered, Milord?

The idea of the king is quickly readable, and only Haniya is simple, even the hub stood up and said:

- There is no further to our spy, and tell him to tell us everything new immediately, with maximum speed.

The king's silence was little understood by the minister:

- Yes, sir.

The concrete weight of the cuffs picked up his clothes, and he left this place, and he runs down, and sent a message to the spy with a dove, flew into space, and the king stood, and he says that his eyes are clear:

- With maximum speed ... not a minute to waste.

Taking thinking over one question is not necessary and is:

"See where the book of the damned is?

Taking think

Preferably

Endless.

* * *

The atmosphere was cool .. The fog thickly spreads everywhere, and in the middle is a Sheikh (Abdullah). He kneels down and feels this lake, which has spread like a haze on the surface. that here and there, and far behind were the ghosts of large and cumbersome approaching, and with them took their features include, screams and what he sees and his eyes stopped in the East and the fall of water from under his fingers and took his heart between ribs, and took the firing squad, he sees as if he was in his place so excited, even with the approach of this knee from him, who considers him to be a creature of larger creatures that he saw her once, it is only seconds until he was not in front of him and next to him, not holding him back bad, strange thing - the more they walk on the surface of the water without worrying about Page Lake !! - He asked himself, surprised at what he saw ?! And his heart trembles with fear, the feeling of the army, the tremendous passage of its members from his side and through him, like a ghost, does not exist, they do not notice that someone asked the same thing !?

- It's true?

I didn't throw an answer, he looks around in front of him until I finish with a knee at the end his back of another creature is so huge that it is gorgeous, but it's strange for the former, Poon of silver and steam from his nose, and there is a donkey on his back, who something did not show his features very well, because he was upstairs and in silence, accepting the passing creature, the silver of his response, but I do not know how to do it. - - - - - -
I signed something on the page of the pond, and in the water in front of the thing they push the thing with their hand into the water and out of this thing quickly, and found my golden mace very in the spirit of the mountains, at the end of it the Black Lily settled among the thorns, taking care of him left and right how he blinded all of his own creation, and suddenly felt someone put a hand on his shoulder, turned around and suddenly found a ghost hiding his features as if completely blurry, increasing the demand from the

organization of his atoms of his body when D is this man's hand with long fingers high that holds the fingers of the dead on a stick. And in the ensuing silence, he left the thing face to face with this unknown person, quickly, like a fly on the ground, rose into the air and flew after him, raising the scepter. To the sky, which thundered violently and the lightning then took the introduction of the cannon wand, little by little the tulips even opened up in the most recently released strong light, blinding the eye, so that the thing could not be seen, but he put his hand over his eyes and shouted, saying:

- My eyes-eyes-Where are you, (burgundy), son?

Accepting the barking of a dog as he looked at the thing, and (burgundy) yelling at the thing, shaking his body of the recorded utterance:

- Uncle woke up ... it's a nightmare.

The hub is a thing from the outdated one that has not been certified! Opening his eyes he said, and he asks:

- Did you turn off the fire, son?

- Never, uncle ... the fire still burns.

D stretched out his hands in front of him and quickly exclaimed:

- (Burgundy) I don't see enough!

And (Burgundy) as if lightning struck him, and exclaimed in frustration:

- What?!

- Exclaimed the old man, and he began to cry, and the words came out trembling. :

- I don't see anything, Mane Amit, son.

And take cheer here: the

- I was blinded.

Annexation (Burgundy) breasts, took the old man screaming and crying, and he hates:

- I was blinded.

Lost my voice in this endless space.

* * *

Taking this spider to vibrate between the leashes, and he watches the Queen of Darkness, she stands in front of a mass of animals in silence, a state of silence dances on a scarf and the appearance of her face, the reflection of this flame was glowing around her, I took the approach of one of them, she said that noticed this and for a long time could not recover.:

"You are finally moving, Tiger Massif.

Then silence ensues, and he watches the drop animal's eyes:

- I thought that this time will never come, but it has come finally and we will receive the book.

The roar of the tiger is huge, opening its mouth so that its fangs are sharp and oil from the lips, whip its neck left and right, Rosa has a half-smile to break the file, he said, and she reared him:

- Wait, kid, take your time; he knew the meaning of the book, and we will all follow him, and nothing can stop us
- exclaimed one of the men accompanying him .:

- Is it true, Milady?

- Yes, that's right; they knew the meaning of the book, and knew exactly where to kiss.

- Where are we going, Your Grace?

- In the most beautiful country, the companies are all their own.

Silence, as you want to add something of value in the modern, quickly said:

- To Egypt.

- To Egypt the Mother of the World and a charming company.

- The guy asked again? He raises an eyebrow to the highest point:

- And where is the reception of the book in Egypt?

An advanced file a step or two forward, said aloud the theater gestures with his hands:

- There among the rocks and mountains in the Egyptian desert.

What is done is more like seeing the seat book followed in Hamas and plodding impatiently, which is a point and into the unknown:

- There the book is waiting for me, I see him, he calls me.

The queen interrupted him suddenly, and I broke her composure and exclaimed that they were looking at the man accompanying him:

- This is Paul calling, he has prepared an iron coup, and let's go to Egypt, Mother of the World.

Go, man behind the wheel, do what I told him. his queen, and hears her muttering, and speaks in a low voice:

- Come on already swim, there the journey to the book is delayed and you will not be accepted.

I thought of her fist and quietly exclaimed:

- It's mine, I'm alone ..

Yes, one - and I will not allow others to get what was, I would pay dearly.

The Queen was an expert in black magic of the damned and always used it to her advantage.

See what will happen in the future?

* * *

The king stood on this large balcony with reliefs and sculptures strange and wonderful at the same time, watching how this waterfall is high, and the lake spreads out like its blue, trees are lush like flowers, Its different colors and shapes.

Stop the file, available to everyone in solemn silence, like in a well of thought, you cannot get out into the world around you, so he feels that the ministry is approaching him, then bend over a little and then quickly think:

"Sorry, sir, but I have urgent news.

I noticed the edges of the folder, after hearing it, I even said without meeting him:

- I moved the Queen with her army and her devotion to the revolutionary iron.

Opening his mouth, the minister exclaimed:

"How do you know, my lord?

"This is just an assumption, Minister, but I cannot guess it. Is there where the level of the book, and where to go to the file with it?

- The minister answered quickly:

- She's heading to Egypt.

He quickly turned the folder towards him and said that he was asking:

- But where is this book in Egypt? It is a large country and very wide.

Catch a kettlebell with your stick and a little salt said:

We told our spy that the book continues in the Eastern Desert, namely on a mountain called (Mountain of the Dead) there is a book in silence.

The fact that I ended as a minister of my speech until I read the pictures to them, and stood waiting in anticipation, and took the king, who saw to see in nothing, taking the weight of the clock with my eyes, it's like waiting to speak until he utters king, and said:

- Tell the cavalrymen that we have an immediate meeting at the round table, this is very important.

The concrete load is the same and, taking his Savior's stick in front of the king, quickly disappeared from sight, and then looked at the file a second time, at the lake and waterfall, and thought, and asked the same thing:

- How is it, the queen of darkness to the book and to?

- How so?

* * *

Hold (Burgundy) - Sheikh (Abdullah) strongly wanted to make it easier for him what happened and asked him

He almost cries crying creature:

- How did it happen, uncle?

He beat the creature on the head and cried. tears streamed down the path from his blind eyes:

- I don't know, son! It must be this nightmare of the damned — that's the reason.

I'm surprised (Burgundy) !! And he exclaimed:

- Any nightmare?

The concrete piece of lapels pulled himself together and sighed deeply, maybe he would be able to accept it and said:

- Yes, I saw a strange nightmare, the knees and ghosts of soldiers and beasts are huge, and -----

Silence of things on the floor, and grabbed the shoulder (tan) from the top said in the importance of giving up what is important for the top, as if to tell him something extremely important:

- I got the folder for the book!

- Faded (burgundy), and his eyes are almost the last, - he quickly asked:

- How do I know?

- I saw them and I guess that the queen knew about us, they brilliantly used black magic, perhaps that is why I lost my sight.

Silence is a thing to swallow your saliva, said the person selling face:

- A nightmare?

- Yes, son, this is a nightmare that I saw.

He did not speak (Burgundian), but carried terror in his heart and to his fear, and the images on both of them were as if cut out in a piece, there is no life in them, only what the dog takes should be advised, but expected
A huge army, the largest army that you see as human beings, and made soldiers with shields and shiny helmets with terrible inscriptions, and in front of the army there was an array of tigers

and they are visible every now and then, and next to them stood two people, one owner of red hair motorcycle thick, and short beard and mustache shaved, another unscrewed the pump of the body, and black hair relaxed behind his clean-shaven face, and in front of the two tigers and the stop of the Tiger, iron puffed steam from time to time, and next to him stood the Queen and she directed her conversation to him. red hair .:

- Ride the tiger, (Cohen), and everything broken will come to you, and do not regret, and do not regret.

He paused and said, looking at the other:

- And you, CEO, do not forget that the word mercy does not exist in our kingdom, destroy everything that you see on our way, and let's get the book at any cost.

Bow (CEO) is a bit like saying yes, while she quickly turns around and grabs the revolutionary iron and focuses on his neck, and settles there until she screams in a harsh voice and they refuse her scepter to heaven , which I took for a whistle and rumbling in force:

- Let's get back to the book and the shabby cloak under our feet, know that this moment will speak of history and will never be forgotten by time, and that there is no place for the faint of heart among us.

She fell silent, and then screamed even louder:

- Do you have the courage?

The bug encourages making cosmic goals of the heart, then they point forward:

- If you are an American forward.

The drums and trumpets of a bug sounded, and an iron bull, then a tiger in the garden, and then the Great Army, which has never seen a world like you ..

And I won't see anything.

* * *

The King sat at this round table, surrounded by a bunch of knights, and they competed in the important at first sight, albeit a little closer, to hear our King say:

- What is the solution now (catfish model)?

He said that a big guy with big muscles and a fluffy heavy beard and mustache is huge:

"What you see is the answer, isn't it, gentlemen?

A tall man, who seemed older, answered, with the small one with gray hair:

- Yes, (catfish model).

The minister was based on reality with a stick next to the king, see attached Said:

- Forgive me, gentlemen, but when would you hear another proposal from an old man like you?

King said he pressed his fingers in front of his face on the table:

- That's what, when the minister can accept him.

It seems, sir, that the Queen of Darkness knew how to keep a black book, and it is meant to ---

The king interrupted him, quickly said:

- Here is the conclusion, Minister, there is no need to waste time.

The minister stutters and says himself, as if the tsar is not interrupting:

- It is suggested to send a small mission up the book quickly, and an easier movement and faster than the queen's army, and you can get rid of the enemies.

The silence of the minister receiving the dog thinks of each other as well, and the King says that he is unbuttoning his fingers:

- What do you say, gentlemen?

Answered by (strand):

"I see that your opinion is correct, Milord.

Added (sum style):

"I can see it, my lord.

And then again and again there, the king exclaimed and said:

- And I like them.

- Since we agreed with this opinion, I would like to say that this mission is optional, it wants to travel, please raise your hand.

The silence of the king burned his eyes as long as he waited for the king, so he thought he would not raise his hand, but suddenly his hand rose (catfish style), and after him came (Strand), and after him more and more, until The last knight, then the king in sweetness and contented with his knights, said as he looked at them with pride:

- We can't all go if we knew the minister's opinion, enough for two, and I will be the second.

- exclaimed the minister and bowed to his king:

- My lord, what are you talking about?

The king answered imperceptibly, but look the riders in the eyes, and he says:

- The minister will return to the Book of honor and pride for any knight, and before I became governor, I am a knight, and in the east I will return to the book and will be a king.

I feel, Minister, that the file is consumed by the level of what he said, he decided to take a back seat while the added file says:

"Do you know who chose you for this dangerous mission?

Everyone shut up fuck and waited for the king in anticipation, and after some silence he said:

- I chose (som model) and (Strand).

Hmm, others, while he smiled at His Excellency on Monday, and may you inflate their egos to the fullest, and the King said, trying to calm everyone:

"Don't grunt inappropriately for knights, you're bigger than that.

Then someone said and was angry and holding his forehead:

- But Sir, we are a sculptor ---

The King interrupted him, saying:

- Do not be sad, everyone has their own roles.

Smile, anger and exclamation:

- Is it true, sir?

"Yes, it's true that the kingdom is here, you must protect and preserve it until I return to find it safe.

Silence the file and then add:

Since the queen has left her kingdom to find the book, you must leave immediately and with maximum speed.

- exclaimed the minister:

"So soon, my lord?"

- Yes, so quickly that she prepared the horses, and prepared supplies, the time for effort has already come, or go back to the book and call him, or ... ---

- First and never come back.

The king spoke these words and did not know that the future holds much up his sleeve for them.

And the ease was the greatest.

The greatest hand of fear ..

Only fear.

* * *

These women flew in transcendental heights, I took spoilage and spun in a circular motion, and below there was (Burgundy) walking next to his horse in this land almost free of life, only a few trees were scattered here and there, and next to him the thing had already left and grabbed the fork, and in the silence he said that after he lost his glint of the eyes, and behind them was to their own damage, that the dog did not suffer a bit.:

- Where are we now, son?

Look (Burgundy) at the map he has, he said, pointing somewhere at it:

- We're next to the valley of buildings.

- If you do not need to go into this fact, and the night comes; I am ashamed of them.

The thing smiled with his saliva and continued:

"Let's go to a safe place to stay overnight, and in the morning we'll be done.

Paint (tan) around him and he will look at the system around him and then exclaim:

- There is a cave, uncle close to the subject.

- Then let me spend the night there, and in the morning we will continue our journey.

The two of them reached the cave, then he (Tang) approached the large stone even closer and silently entered the cave and the floor.

* * *

Taking these three Musketeers to plunder the plundered land, not to commit or eat, neither sleep, nor even forge ahead, he insisted that the Queen and now accelerate with them to summon the army of the Queen, and walked past through the green valleys, with high grasses , with white birds flying all over the place, and forests of trees, and tall branches intertwined, and a desolate plain, until they reached a high plateau, and then they stood at the edge of it, looking at the green valley below, and looked at those horses, spread out in the library under the shade of palm trees, and that was very good. the small lake was a figment of the imagination, he smiled at the king and said in sweetness:

- Finally we got to the land of the Nile.

Silently, he closes his eyes, then takes a deep breath to feel the women and say:

- Since childhood, I dreamed of visiting this land, I heard about a miracle.

Then he opens his eyes and adds:

- I know that he is no longer there, and by the smell of heaven.

"Let's go down to this land and look at its soil, and at the Queen of the Dark Army.

His friends are stung by the smile and the consequences of falling from this plateau in speed, and they all hope that it is in the King and his army.

How it was hope.

* * *

From afar and on this high mound stood a group of children gathering some wild plants, and during this I heard one of the children, with a voice coming from the distant horizon, stop what he was doing and looked at the horizon, and suddenly my eyes it somehow strangely expanded and shook with every cell, and exclaimed:

- Listen ... is this the army or I don't see?

The children stopped looking at the horizon, and one of them said in surprise:

- Oh my God, what is it ?! This is the largest army I have ever seen.

Taking the children, we look in silence, as if those who have turned into statues are lying and the women are fluttering their clothes, and suddenly one of the children loses his composure, then starts down the hill and shouts straight without stopping:

- A huge army is marching towards, like locusts.

Here, all the children scream like you and scatter along all the streets of the village, and if someone hears this, even enters his house and closes the doors and windows, then the state of noise inside the village, which soon reached the army of darkness, like a fly on the ground , and here the queen spoke clearly and rudely, like a demon, not a man:

"They destroyed everything in this village, let's leave our mark wherever we get to it, and leave a stone unturned, but destroyed it.
And to hear the members of the army that so they set out to witness the decay everywhere, and the bug in the air kept screaming and screaming, and took the children everywhere, both women and men, and took home a corkscrew under the feet of the army, and in just a few minutes until everything calmed down, he chose the village from existence, taking the army smiling and leaving behind the remains of the village that was in this place once.

* * *

When he entered (Burgundy) and she fell into the cave from a group of stones, suddenly closing the entrance completely, understand the thing quickly:

- What's happening?

-This is an entrance, uncle, I think we drove into the gas valve at some time?

Silence (Burgundy) as he looked at the rocks that completely blocked the entrance to the cave, then added:

- What now?

- exclaimed the one whom he took on his stick, which was leaning against it, and raised his face up .:

- Tell me, Sonny, now you have sight, can we move this stone away from the entrance?

- He's too big, uncle.

- So let's look for another way out.

Silence is such a thing as if it was thinking about something and then said:

- Look around, son, and tell me what you see.

- The cave is very big, uncle, so big that the ceiling is very high, it was a sign that things are being divided, drops of water are falling.

- Are these things low white?

- Yes, pretty much white.

- This is urgent, this is the cave you fall into ... this is the complete set.

- The cave is lit with dim lighting, making it easier for her to see.

- If you look around for a way out of this light.

Taking (tan) looked for some way out of this cave clearly, and suddenly screamed in a loud voice, as if a scorpion had bitten him .:

- Uncle ..

Ruffled thing, and the hub stood up and exclaimed:

- Have you found anything, son?

- Yes, uncle, there is a tunnel at the end of his world.

He said what he is trying to get around the sound source:

- Come on if we skip this butter.

Catch the (Burgundian) sheikh (Abdullah) by the hands and move him and the floor in front of you, wagging his tail, and behind him the creature moves linearly until it reaches the end of the tunnel, the creature said when you stop:

- Have you reached the end, son?

- Yes, uncle.

- Why is the tone so sad, son?

"We entered another cave of about the same size and with the same compositions and details.

- Do not despair, son, I am sure that God will not leave us, and I feel that we are already near the exit, in sha Allah, we will go here or there.

The left (upper) hand of the aunt, starting to look for the second time, and all this is Hamas, and then not so long ago I did not find out anything, and he turned to sit next to his aunt, said in frustration:

- I could not find anything, it seems that something was written in this damn place.

His patience speaks of a pat on the back:

- Do not despair at the mercy of God, God is more than anything else.

- And yes to God.

Silence on Monday and stretched the floor in front of them, and the three in majestic silence and seconds passed, as if eons are endless, and taking the demon of amateur photography with a terrible head (Burgundy) and not reaching this place, and during this interaction the black watchdog for what - then he raised his ears up, then raising his head gave out that it was necessary to take strongly, as he looked at the wall on which the thing was based (Burgundy), out of curiosity raised his last head and saw where the floor in question was, immediately exclaimed in surprise thing:

- Son, what is it?

There was no answer (Burgundy), but preferred the sound, as if from surprise he loses his sense of pronunciation, and the sound is the barking of dogs that do not pass by

Taking leaves in Genappa cave but stopped

It is determined

Determined.

* * *

Session file (wise) said in front of the people, and they took turns in the things of the kingdom and ordered the book and did not notice how these eyes are brooding and approach them in quiet silence, until they stopped next to them and they made a pad, and behold I feel like the king of their existence interrupted the conversation and kept silent, prompting (catfish style) to say:

- Sir, what's the matter?

The sharpened file did not shock, but whispered:

- Get ready, it looks like our guests are not welcome.

The king stood calmly and his friends, and with their backs to every stop they stopped and prepared to meet what was coming, and the owners of these eyes slowly closed and growled from time to time, until the clapping became frightening, they became a group of Wolves, black and gray creepy, when it's next.

They advanced in a slow, terrible movement, one after another, and oil dripped from their Achilles tendons, the community looked at the abandoned horror in the hearts of the most powerful people, showed their sharp fangs, and in the silence from behind the king's back he used his weapon with my blade for its pumping, as did (Strand) (som model) and their weapon-ax, its huge blade and Hammer rail is huge, and the rules of the group to attack the ferocious wolves and passed moments to follow the staff, they provide the strength of each of them. as long as the soil, as it were, stood them at the moment, and there the king said that he was watching the creepy eyes:

"Don't worry about them, let them attack first, and no matter what happens, don't break the ranks.

(The Strand) exclaimed excitedly:

- Where did all these monsters come from?

Smile (catfish model) in mock, saying ::

"It doesn't matter where they came from, but it's important to live after they leave this place.

It was such a terrible moment for everyone, and they expected an attack at any moment, but meanwhile, the difference between the Wolves is a huge wolf, he is all black, and they are at a slow pace, like their leader, and in silence for our heroes, and suddenly a grimace of fangs and a loud howl and seemed to know about the beginning of dinner, a friendly line and wolves are coming at you from all sides and from all sides with frightening speed and mortal danger .:

- We fought with the greatest courage, and our life is in our hands to walk easily.

Was the act of the Wolves abnormal, was the organization so large, attacked, some of them took the king to protect themselves and took the bodies of the Wolves falling like flies around him, and taking (catfish style) overturns and legs without pause or respite, and taking (a strand) breaks all the bodies that held them and had hot blood on their faces, and it seemed that the battle would never end, and with this everything stopped and the king was breathing heavily due to his efforts, it was the same case with mine friend, and clearly (catfish style) Blood on his face, he said, still looking at the many wolves who silently looked at him .:

- Are we done?

The file that the wolf is watching the president answered:

- It looks like we have not finished yet, the second round is underway.

I didn't have time to finish the Art Nouveau file, so the second round began faster than the perception of beauty, and it looks like this round is fiercer than they expected, it increased the number of wolves nearby and became more ferocious, and death went bloodthirsty between their fangs ---

The blood is fresh and warm.
I took the folder to the page of this very pond, in which the moonlight was reflected and the image of the stars in silence, in the silence of tigers, someone armed to the teeth came up, and if necessary, until he stood behind her completely, before doing what -or movement, she told him that the folder was still in place .:

What brings you here at this hour?

Sayid, trying to control the lapels, pulled himself together and, sitting next to Linda, tells her:

- Ma'am, I've never seen her .-----

I interrupted him and she raised her hand in front of his mouth and said in a wide wonderful voice, free from any emotion:

"I know what to hide ... there is no need for frequent conversations, (Cohen), provided you make an effort to speak to you.

A little closer to her, so that his breath was warm, I bumped into her face and whispered like a snake from hell:

- You know that I ... ---

Silence to swallow his saliva in extreme difficulty, and encouragement continued:

- I'm in love with you ?!

I did not speak to the Queen until she was silent, and thought about her owner and the fact that whole epochs passed in minutes of silence, which he said again:

"I'm sure you know that I am the Savior, the only one here who wants nothing but your love, I want to stand next to you, to see you until the end of time.

The king's silence once again did not comment on his words, but I asked the same question:

Also over the years, the person in him has not touched me ??
In indecision, he grabbed the queen's palm and kissed her lightly, and she found herself melting next to him, at that moment I forgot that she was the queen, and that this was one of her followers, and reproduced all the muscles of her body, attacked her with another like a hungry lion devours its prey ..

Yes, his prey.

It was two steps from the eyes, and the moon did not follow them.

Yes, only the Moon.

* * *

Stop this white knight, watching the entrance to the cave, closed by rocks, suddenly the melted guide through the horse quickly took him and owned the car until he got to him, fell from the back of the horse and grabbed the stones, as if he wants to open the entrance to the cave in the second time, but after a while he fizzled out and honored him with breathing and profuse sweat, and sat on the stones with his chest, and knows the goals of the intensity of the efforts that he applied to this, and seconds passed, and his eyes rotated in their sockets, and then stopped, as crazy and began to try to open them. Once again, it was not possible to knock out the stones ..

He returned the ball a second time, and the failure was his ally.

Accepting the fight without a fight, but each time failing, for he is very large and numerous, and in the end, after many attempts, he fell on his back from an overabundance of fatigue and effort, as if he succumbed to this end, so tears left his eyes, and did not understand, that from the search, how we are still alive inside the cave, and did not imagine one day that he would meet them again in this life, and accepted crying, it seems, taking with his head buried in the center of his palms next to his horse, which silently watched him and behind the flying locks of hair., his weight, which pulled at his neck.

* * *

We take a file corresponding to these wolves, with unparalleled courage, and with the continuation of the Battle they took the strong, everyone weakened little by little, the wolves did not stop attacking, instead of killing them, ten came, while everyone thought that victory would be inevitable for the wolves, I took their number, to multiply so that some could have access to the leg (strands) from the back, and thrust sharp fangs into flesh and warm blood.

And they hit him (the workers) with a powerful blow on his campaign from the spot and threw away the fallen dead body, and when she saw that the wolves rushed with blood on him, wounding him in the thigh and chest and nearly falling between them, but he took his the gun left and right, not stopping, and he gasped, dizzy from too much blood loss.

Noticing (catfish-style) from his place what is happening with a friend and dealing with him quickly and taking the defender valiantly and with the utmost strength and cruelty, take the dead one and kill every wolf that approaches them, like a machine made only to during the respite of this battle, the garrison was attacked by a wolf, which plunged claws into his back and screamed (soma-style) strongly from the pain he felt at this terrible moment, and opened the wolf's mouth with its tail, sharp fangs and oil falling from his lips and then hit the shoulder (catfish-style) brutally blood explodes like an erupting volcano.

And he tried to throw him off his shoulder, but the pain was very strong, held him and was his friend, and so they bred the Wolves, his ferocious and his friend, the king noticed in what happened, tried to help them and them, but a lot of them prevented him from getting before them, the order to defend himself, he jumped one on his chest and thrust one of his claws into it, and it was enough that she also tried to bite his shoulder, and he succeeded, and took the king's blood to the ground, and wolves from all sides and from all sides, like waves that never end.
Taking the king, he tried to defend himself, but he fell in the end, he fizzled out down his body from the thickets all efforts were directed to the very defense, and the stars that shone in the sky and wolves grew up, you see, the stars appeared with sharp fangs, and The king realized that death is going between these fangs, he tried to finish, but he no longer feels his body, he completely relaxed, tried to resist the disease, but failed in his attempt, and the difficult and terrible moments passed, but something strange happened !!

I calmed down, all of a sudden !! As if there is someone who will stop them, stop them ?! In the worlds allowed by the file worlds, the wolf appears, and only a few seconds pass until it disappears, all the wolves from where it came from, as if they were not there for a few moments, are surprised that nothing happened to the king ?! He did not even believe that he got up in great difficulty, and saw how the owner (catfish model) tried it with another advance, proceeded to the steps filled with stress and fatigue, spread over his body with wounds, and took blood dripping from them incessantly, and stopped even before the owner told him:

- Are you okay, buddy?

He answered the call and said about some kind of operation on his arm:

- I think so, it is important to live.

Here the king asked:

- Where is the owner of the second?

- Of course, here or there.

And when they heard two weak voices, they realized that the owner was lost, and he, looking for him, found him, was distributed by an outstanding surgeon, he did not file bows quickly, and looked at the face of his owner, which selected his features were completely under the blood of blood red colors, he said after I quickly examined his body:

- Do not be afraid, brave as a result, your not an adult, do not worry, but you are tired and hyper, that you are defending yourself from his efforts, champion.

Silence of the king and k (catfish style) and told him ::

"We have to stay here during the day to eat to heal these wounds, and even a friend is free to talk to us.

Exclaimed (strand) that is in the severity of pain

- No, no, no, no time, you go.

The king said:

"Don't talk now, I won't leave you, whatever the results.

Try (strand) to say something, but the king put his finger to his mouth to signal health, they say (som style :)

- It's amazing that wolves also came and went !!!

The king said:

"I don't know, but it seems they are not ordinary, they are fascinated by the charm of what, we don't know who cut the tension rope between the wolves and the owner of the magic, of course, something strange is happening around us.

Full (catfish style :)

- This is troubling.

Cutter (strand) word weak:

- Will the wolves work again?

Answer (catom style :)

- Don't even think about it, my friend, and make sure that there is no end yet, and there is still time to see where the new life and the New Day of Inshall are, even if only for a few hours, roll the air, now it is important to use your health.

It was the sound of each until they looked at each other in a fugue they asked themselves:

"See I sent this to the wolves? What else awaits us?

The answer was frightening in its entirety - and confusing.

* * *

- This fox creature started quickly, as if frightened by something in the very heart of this tubular cave, its faint light appeared at the end, and suddenly a hand appeared, as if it had come out of the ground, and I grabbed onto that part of the floor, the back of my head (wine) and tried to raise his body in difficulty, even climbed to the floor of this cave temple, then bent down to quickly draw what was to him, and he fell on his back, breathing heavily from overexertion of efforts, uttered an intermittent word:

- We finally arrived, I thought that I could all my life with this wall.

In the meantime, (Burgundy) was, holding his dog in his arms, said:

- As long as God is with us, do not be afraid, sir, nothing.

The dog nervously barked his hand at the entrance to the cave, the cave is so narrow that no one is allowed to park, Rainbow (wine) is on his stomach and said to his uncle:

- Come on, sir, let's get out of here, I can almost feel him choking.

Answer the question:

- Do you see any way out in front of you, son?

- Yes, I see it ... walking outside, it turns out their close party.

Silence (burgundy) and the director said:

"Follow me, sir, they grabbed me and pushed me behind my back.

Indeed, the creature was crawling behind him, and the article contained a dog that, seeing the fox, ran away from its place, and the minutes that passed suddenly stopped (burgundy) from the crowd, and this creature became worried:

- Why did you stop, son?

- In fact, nothing but an invented annoying idea.

- What's the matter?

"What if (A.J.) calls him first to make a reservation? How will the situation turn out?"

- Don't think about anything, my son hasn't happened yet, so I'm not learning to negotiate, let's do what we have to do to get a kiss, she quickly put one thing in your head, this is that we are all our strength to get an accepted book.

Look (burgundy) bed said:

- When you really are, uncle.

- Then hurry up and do not waste time, there is a long way ahead.

Quickly taking out (the wine) we crawl out, and we get to the director's performance in his head outside, and when he did it, he tore off something very peeping !! Even he could not say anything or warn the aunt who took Polzunov, this is called:

- (Burgundy) where are you, son?

- And I have not received any answer to his question ..

- The building where you are is falling to pieces, but he hears nothing except the constant barking of a dog.

Here's a thing dude:

- What's going on here?

- The sound was terrifying, there is the silence of a word in it, the silence is like the silence of graves, and it took the very heart of the thing

Must be wildly non-stop, so it's almost horrifying.

* * *

A knight in a mask, a tail, the clothes of a white horse galloped, and set off aimlessly, and being fast without stopping, until he heard the consequences of the wolf, and saw a pack of wolves walking in front of him and saw their role, marveled at her !! Out of curiosity, he followed them, and stopped over one of the hills, and over a tree (sycamore) Stopping high, the knight saw this terrible fight between wolves and three men, marveled at his audacity and courage !! And suddenly the moment of the Wolves came, and they went from where they came from, and saw that the surgeon had the second thickener, and he spoke at the stand, and so he decided to kill them even with respect to their personality, taking the tigers sneaking into Hefei, and approaches , and approaching silently i-Hefei.

* * *

Take the salt, heal the owner's wounds to the beat, and then suddenly watch what is coming from behind these bushes, stop what he was doing, he said, referring to (som style :)

- It seems to me, my friend, that we are not alone in Palma, it all comes down to one.

Panic attacks (strand) exclaimed that his eyes widened:

- Do you usually have wolves?

"Don't worry, this is not a Wolf Movement, he is human.

- exclaimed (catfish style :)

- huh? And what does he want this asshole

"I don't know ... that's what we want to know if we should continue what we did so that we don't find out that we knew about it and had it."

The silence of the three, and in order to give traces with the tip of the eye, moves this ghost from tree to tree, and approaches them more and more, so much so that the king can easily catch up with him with them, here the king gallops on his horse like lightning, throws an arrow at the ghost, who threw his legs in the wind, but the horse was faster, he quickly approached him, and now the king jumped off his horse to catch up with her, and both fell to the ground.

Throw the last one away from the king, who rolled to the side, then the hub of reality, quickly, here showing the form of a ghost, he is a white knight, and quickly straighten reality by pulling a double-edged whip in the air from behind your back, as a warning sign indirectly to the king that a naked sword is behind the other, and the two around each other, and then attacked two and came up with swords, and took a leaf line in the air, taking two combat skills, a file look to my eyes, the rider when approached and found a ghost smile in his eyes , said he believes in one of his blows:

- It will look more when I remove the colon, Slick malignant.

I did not speak to the white knight, but continued to hit him with a strip non-stop, and the attack of the king in a rage intensified to strike him with force, and the other was done brilliantly, like no other, and then the king again said:

"I don't know where you learned to defend and fight like that ?! But I'm pretty sure you knew that this fearless knight is not afraid to die and does not understand the meaning of fear.

Book of the Damned Episode 6 (Terrible Trouble)
The king fought in a fierce battle with this stubborn knight, and the clash of swords sparkled
The White Knight said to ward off the king's blow on one of his swords lying on his back, then skillfully and quickly looked behind the back of the file, and grabbed the sword last to put it in the king's back, but the king was skilled in defense and attack, so he jumped with an acrobatic jump arranged him behind the knight, turned around and the last one quickly decided to hit the king's feet, bringing the king to Earth, and before returning to Earth he quickly stumbled over a stone and stopped, and the knight took advantage of this opportunity, and tried to pay off him. blow, but King Echo quickly and quickly began to fall again, I took the swords to release sparks in all directions, and took the movement of defense and attack between the two to take on the nature of a secret, and suddenly the king jumped On the knight, and stop on the ground, and settle the king higher chest, knight and face to eyes, and the king discovered that there was something strange in the eyes of this masked knight, so much so that he forgot himself,

and now you see the knight on his chest, you see that he does something after of how he lost his sword.

I decided to run, but the king grabbed him by the leg and said:

- Are you going to find out the secret of these eyes?

Try the knight with your stubbornness to leave, but he could not, and at that moment (catfish model) appeared and said in his hoarse voice:

- What's going on here?

At the stops, the knight turned out of his own and looked at him, and the file took advantage of this opportunity and quickly pulled the hooded knight's Balaklava to itself, and there was a surprise ?! - He exclaimed and opened his eyes wide. :

- Boss !!

- Girl? !!

And it was a surprise to the king (cat style !!)

* * *

Kill one to follow the Queen of Darkness, and quickly approach her tent and exclaim:

- Milady, there a young man with a dog came out of the cave, the camp is around him, and ...

And he did not finish his speech, but stood surprised, looking at his leader (Cohen), who was lying on his stomach with a strip of a large portion !! His signs of fear intensified when he looked into the case, and seconds passed, and then he looks at the bottom of it, as if there is something there, and his eyes do not believe the words that say:

- Where did I go to S ---

He did not finish his speech, but he completely completed the dossier of one employee, so that her porcelain face was in its place and said:

- Catch everyone coming out of the cave, there is something that unites us.

- Bowing to the situation and quickly leaving the tent, he concreted (Cohen) his clothes, and he got up and decided to ask her something in his head ..

But she said no and gave it back .:

- Don't ask how it happened? You know much less how it happens.

- The withered (Cohen) felt that the queen behind her mountain was standing high, almost to the sky and the size of a small ant ... and then I followed him .:

"Get out now, and I was sure that if someone found out what happened here, they would bite your tongue before you even opened your mouth.

- Silence from the Silence of them all, so that (Yazbek) stopped staring at her back like a statue, and looked for a long time, then bowed his head and, perhaps, felt that his size was very small and insignificant in comparison with him, and wrote several steps from the tent, and before he reached her door, the queen stopped him, and she tells the guide about snakes and demons:

- Oh, I forgot to tell you something

Stop where you are, as if he could hear, then slowly raised his head and looked at him.

And without sticking to it or considering it said:

- I had the most wonderful day.

- And that he said these words until I looked at him and met my eyes, and looked at him with some horror and fear, and the people there smiled, disappearing behind this porcelain mask, then left her and left the stage, and fear of them filled his heart after he loved her.

* * *

Creeping creature (Abdullah) until I feel the air kiss his forehead, and I feel around me, and I lift my head up, and I hear a dog barking from afar, Do not be afraid:

- Built-in - where are you? RSVP

So he grabbed one in his palm and pulled it, suffered from this oil, and when he heard the (burgundy) sound of something screaming:

- Hey rats, leave him alone. he is the Sheikh of the pyramid.

- The creature shouted, and he grabbed her by the neck and said anxiously:

- Of these, (tan) is there?

Someone roughly punched him in the side and said:

"Don't ask, old man.

Try (burgundy) to get rid of them, he said, shouting at the top of his voice:

- How dare you do that when at a very old age you cannot stand up for yourself? Come out, said, as strong as you, pig.

The other guy laughed and bared his teeth and said yellow:

"What if we gave you enough time to basically pray to God to see the sun tomorrow, you are a brave hero.

The laughter of all the people around him is in savages and they are a thing and so on, and his owner screams as he tries to slip away from them and scream:

- Come on beast.

The dog is behind him, being by his neck and he was supposed to be a Cord, but he did not care about the men or the owner or the boho of our sheikh, and after a while they all stood in front of the queen, sat on her throne in her face. ceramics said:

- What a young and beautiful face, a strong body, I would like to know ... who are you? And where did you come from? This is not your father or your dog.

Without an answer, but taking pictures of them, and looked at him, and looked into his eyes, and then pointed at her with his palm, and she said:

- I don't like this answer, but you don't need to hear it, because I know everything about you.

Silence then she said mischievously:

- O (Burgundy)

Surprised (Burgundy) and what! And the dog seems to understand what is happening around it, beats its (Burgundian) head energetically and tells you to read the same:

- This must be the same nightmare. !! I'm delirious, delirious, delirious .---

Overall, the file looks simple:

- But you really live, you do not need to be yourself.

Silence of dogs, thing lifted, head up, he said, gripping his stick .:

- Look, Phoenix has been living for thousands of years, and her disciples are always and always to the East.

- I interrupted him, - said the King angrily, - Khader already understood what he meant .:

"Take this old man and the dog, put them in the bone prison, which they themselves put on it.

Silence said they were used to her tent:

- You will complete the journey with us, our goal is one.

The dog knows the target is the book.

Yes, the Black Book.

* * *

- Stop file is not certified and has not been seen !!! A girl of great beauty who was not at all (Lilina's) sister (Burgundian) and was hiding behind this white veil, and when I look at the file, so that the color of her eyes melts in mercy, like a lump of sugar that melts among a cup of hot tea, a lump in sea air, taking a dive into the depths, and trembles, and only the sound (catfish style) saves, he shouts ::

"Don't let the snake's smoothness kill you by surprise, my lord.
- Follow the king of speed !! It was found that (Lilia) took out one pig, was installed in the leg, and was the king in a sneak strike, so the use of two captures saw each other in a challenge, and suddenly (Lily) pulled out a sword was fastened behind her back, and struck them up ... then the king stood in his place motionless, then he tried to beat him, but he (catfish style) grabbed his sword heavily and parried the blow (Lily) in strength, but it looked like a circus, was seized by his rebuff and jumped into the air, and concentrated on her arms, and buried her body in the air to meet the full cycle after the core of her body, and landed behind him, the wave hit her near his feet, but he jumped up so quickly and attacked her neck with his sword, but escaped the blow, She was on her back to back with utmost flexibility, and jumped back Dan while standing screamed and she attacked him, and did not look at the wound in the shoulder, so the thin thread of blood was hot and he looked at his wound and said a reward to the fangs in anger, said he, gripping the hilt of the sword in force almost at hand:

"You are not a simple girl, but you are a demon of content, and I will show you now how to fight the cavalry?"

-She smiled at the irony of fate, and the murder of her master is more than a shout, and he threw them, he became angrier and sharper, and began to respond to him with blows with extreme speed and cruelty, but she was very good at retaliating, as if slowly, and suddenly I took the blow with the utmost speed and strength, made him step back and did not notice this stone that was sitting behind him, and during the retreat he stumbled over him and balance, and he fell on his back, and I took advantage of (Lily) the ability to add a sword to his neck, call the file:

- No, please, I don't want to lose him.

From time to time (Lily) looked at him a little hesitantly, and people from the position of the king told him:

Maybe he poses a solution to this problem, he fell in love with her ... leave him alone, and trust me, I will not cause you any trouble.

In all their fullness, you will receive from hyper the efforts that you made in this struggle:

"How do I know you're not going to trouble me again?

"I swear on my honor.

- Two seconds, and (the sum of the model) is visible to the eyes of (Lily) and she looks at him, and then takes out the same hot Said:

- You have another opportunity to see tomorrow morning.

- Here, the implementation (of the catfish style) breathed a sigh of relief not to put swords on his neck, and moved away from him to shake the king, who told him:

- I (sage) come from a distant country.

"She looked into his eyes, and she felt not a shock, but a surprise that something inside her was calling her to check," she told him simply and affectionately:

- I'm (Lily) from here.

- The tsar did not have peace for a long time and she felt the warmth of her hand, pulling the tip of the paper from under his fingers, and said:

- I think that a gentleman like you will not come out of this world, a girl is weak like you.

- The King faded and exclaimed:

- How do you know that I am a nobleman?

"Your clothing, sir, indicates that it looks like an angel's.

I have not heard the sound of Monday (som model) and he says sarcastically:

"The girl is weak, say the demons from the demons of hell.

She (Lily) made her raise one eyebrow and the tip of her eye:

- You say something like that?

Looking at her in anger and lifting the corner of his lips, he said, pressing on his teeth:

- Never say anything.

He said that he was sitting next to him on one of the logs:

"Forget it and let me get to know you better.

Silently swallowing saliva and looking at her forehead, An said:

- What are you doing, skinny, in this wilderness?

She felt comfortable next to him, she felt safe in front of modern stoicism, in front of the appearance of his Malihi, so I decided to tell him my story, and he began to listen carefully, and now and then raised an eyebrow of the doctoral student in horror at what he heard, wondering at the king about this and deciding not to distract him with her book, she could have stayed with him instead of leaving him and the city, cleansed of what happened to her brother, and told him:

- I do trade and travel to many countries), Agama, Arabs and India (both weird and even stranger, and I watched the horrors of what happened to the fetuses inside their mother's belly, though, so I love to travel a lot, and today we were attacked by a pack of wolves and my friend was with me, who hurt the third wolves and the opening of the depression is extremely.

- And what did you do with him?

- Nothing?

- Can I see it?

- Let's go and show you.

- The two of them quickly left, and behind them (catfish style), who became interested in their words and growls. He kicks the ground with indignation, even all disappeared from the office.

* * *

Quietly taking the sun disk, timidly crawling out of the trees, I chose the birds of the sky and recognized their sounds, and I could not hear the screams of some crows, which now and then flew away to a monotonous and dull and distant place .. The back of the Dark Army is preparing for a campaign, offers this revolutionary iron to my queen, who took a look from behind the mask of her horizon, and the desecration of a smile on her face, and behind her was a tiger array and to them, in the back of the cage was a large one with a picture of a (Burgundy) and a dog, grabbed Burgundy pipe, and took the next position in silence, and, taking the horn to go shouts between then and then, drums beat, black banners that paint on the shape of the queen's mask as a symbol of the king, and fluttering crosswise in the air, took the floor, speaking slowly, and then the Sheikh asked:

- The structure we're talking about, right?

- Yes, uncle ..

The dog barked in force, as if it knew about his presence, he accompanied her on his head and said:

- Calm down, my friend.

The creature exclaimed:

- How you threaten the prisoner, son!

- When you are confident in God that we will succeed in Insha Allah, this generation is scary, and as soon as possible.

Raise this thing to the very top of his head and his nose for air will say:

- Where are we going today?

"I heard the words hesitate between them as we head into the valley of buildings.

This thing exclaimed was the lightning of his wound:

- Valley of buildings !!!

I quickly turned to him (Tang) when he heard the tone of what he said to him:

- Yes, uncle, what scared you so?

- Do you know what is in the valley of buildings?

- And what's in there?

- There is no time to explain, but let me first tell them, otherwise we are all doomed

And then he shouted loudly:

- Stop it ... we will all die if we enter the structures of the valley in the morning.

And the word is loud and echoes with barking, and the scream has lost its voice among the voices of the drums that beat without stopping, and the scream (Cate Blanchett) too, but hey, the drums sound on top of them, and took the army going non-stop like they were nothing do not hear, and the view from the back of the valley buildings, everything from the skeletons of various creatures died a long time ago, the bones are white unblemished, and the view there seems to be something terrible between the flanks of this fact.

Everything carries the meaning of death.
He threw the sun, then his golden rays on that (Lily) and trade (strand), whose wounds were bleeding terribly, and asked her for a file, he looks at her with admiration:

- Do you have experience in teaching me?

I did not speak, but looked at the surgery (Strand), and then I stopped and quickly looked around, and at some plants, and plucked a few leaves, and took a good look at her, then put it back on her palm, and put it on the surgery (Strand) , and before touching him, he grabbed her hand (model catfish) and put it in a backpack .:

- What are you going to do, and will it be in this case after he finally loses consciousness?

I looked at her hand and raised my eyebrows to show that she was looking into his eyes:

- You hurt me ..

After a moment's silence, her left hand looked into her eyes and said:

"Don't do anything until you tell us what you are going to do with this poor fellow.

- You do not trust me?

- How to trust a girl who fights with men and skillfully wields cavalry? So we have known each other for only a few minutes.

I felt (Lilia) that he embarrassed her with his words, these, as he said, nervous:

- You're right, anyway, you just have no one to help.

Taking her hand in inspiration, the king quickly grabbed her hand and said, trying to defuse the situation:

- (Sum model) is not intended to offend you.

Far away in his proofs, it is said, moves to look into the eyes of the King, who watch warily to the right:

- Then what does he mean?

They (catfish style) said something angrily, But the King stopped him with a gesture of his hand and said:

- If my friend said what he said according to the logic of his fear of his master, then this is not an excuse.

Then he reached out a little and hit him with the tips of his fingers to her face until I became her eyes before his eyes, said sweetly that he was painting a thin smile on his face:

- And then the amnesty is returned.

She smiled and on her face she read the same request? What is this strange connection that connects them to (wise), and it makes her heart beat wildly every time I look into his eyes ?! And the smile of Walter running to the newspapers speaks of Grande (catfish style), which I took from smoke, anger (catfish style) than a watch, and exclaimed in anger, rumbling ::

- And what are you doing!

She looked at him in silence ... and saw the King shake his head, stretch, continuing what she was doing, here is the first:

- You go to kill your people, sire, this is -----

Quickly the King put his hand on the mouth (catfish model) of existence on his deathbed, noted (Lily) what had happened, I quickly looked at them and found that the king was smiling and saying:

- Keep doing what you do and forget about that whiner.

She turned around to continue her work, and immediately dragged the owner away, created a place and gagged him in time, another said.

- What are you doing, Milord?

- Shut up, dumbass. and tell me no more, Milord, that I am now a merchant, and you are helping me, have you forgotten?

- Why all this?

- Something in me; I don't want to know my real self now.

And suddenly!! I heard her voice coming from behind their backs .:

- You, like, closed your conversation in secret?

- exclaimed the King:

- How long have you been here?

She said no and gave it back and left:

"Don't be afraid, and I've never heard anything from them.

The king sighed and said:

- Thank God .

Were surprised (summed up) the sayings of the king and his actions !! And for B (Layla) to close (strand) followed them (soma style), and there is an unexpected area, and make them stand staring at the two in front of them !! So the king approached slowly and took turns becoming a knight, while the wide eyes (catfish model) said he was surprised:

- So you're a witch !! And you know it.

The furious shouted:

- Watch your language, this ... and do not go over more than your right to the right of another.

The king said that he is in the power of a miracle:

- I wonder how you did it ?! There are no traces of wounds at all.

She (Lily) just:

- The whole interpretation, and this is not the only sign, but the secret from the secrets of the ancients, taught to me in earnest, was a miracle in medicine, this is just one of his recipes, and there is no such treatment there; it makes wounds disappear quickly and on time, and stimulates the skin to simply reproduce.

Exclaimed (catfish style) that refers to the index finger:

"But this is magic and juggling.

The dude says that he held her forehead:

- Do you like looking at magic?

- Come on, show me your real self.

She felt at that moment that she made the mistake of saying It, deciding to quickly change her position, she said:

- If not enough, then a knight. - - - - -

I stutter and say again:

"If that wasn't enough, your partner will stop pestering me.

- The king exclaimed, as if he had not only heard the last phrase.

- No, no, please stay with us.

Review (som model) he said it with his forehead:

- Sir, you -----

- Shut the fuck up and stop chasing her.

They approached the king and told him:

"I hope you don't mind this happening.

I didn't know, but the strand quickly caught everyone's attention and they said (Som style :)

- He seems to be waking up ..

She (Lily) in secret:

- Will be, but will not restore full performance only after a period of rest.

- Asked the king .:

- How long is this period?

- Not less than a day.

Here is the said file to read the same:

"But that will make us too late for our onward journey.

And the King knows that this delay may be in the real master of them !! And nobody knows what will happen in the future ?? This is the hand of God ..

Yes, however, one God.

* * *

I put an iron bull, one of his lists on this skeleton, screw by screw, and with each step she moved thousands of buildings that stretched out in this valley as dense as a mass grave, and the crevice of the valley between the two mountains, and the Army of Darkness crawled to the inner side fact in a slow and measured movement, and everyone saw the skeletons scattered by the tournament fact with surprise and terrible fear creeping into the hearts of every step !! I took the crows that croak in an annoying voice, the rest are on the side of my fact, and I took some soldiers watching the crowds of crows, and they look with concern opaquely at the end of the valley, and it is a pity that the end was not closer than this, and then while he took the horses that experience the cage of the great leap to the top, like her touch of madness, and her owner tried to control her and dragged her into what she crane, took to beat her with whips until they bend around him and get angry, silent everything, even the drums are silent and only the sound of the Ravens' voice destroyed structures that did not belong, and during this he said (Burgundy) He grabbed the bars of the cage and the broken structures .:

- This is a fact only of a cemetery and a large distribution in buildings of all shapes and floors.

What has been said is in a state of indescribable horror and fear:

"I hope to get out of here safe and sound, and between this terrible reality, otherwise you decorate these structures, another group has come here to die in silence.

- What happened to the owners of these structures to die here in this reality ??

"Matt, my son is in terrible pain.

- Have you been to this valley, uncle?

- Never, my son, and I do not have the heart to enter it, but there they told me, warned me about it.

- And the secret is that she needs this reality?

Silence this thing a little ... - as if he wants to add even more fear to his conversation, - he said aloud.

"This is the worst image ... this is death in life.

Passing the deer between them, but one thing hasn't shut up yet, namely the voice of the crushed structures under the wheel cage is great, up there on the Tigris the array said (Sioux) brotherhood:
- But what about the valley of the melancholic?

Added by his colleague (Cohen), saying:

- Believe me, Honey. structures scattered on every stone and in every place.

- It seems that this fact is only the graveyard of the greats.

- What do you mean by that?

"Nothing, dear brother, but it seems that the end is nearer than I imagined.

- Where does the end come from?

- Don't bother yourself, I sometimes say anything about anything, don't bother yourself with talking, buddy.

Put (Cohen) on his lips after this conversation, after a period of silence he said:

- See if we will reach the end of this terrible fact?

A reputation (SEO) question, but he could not guarantee an answer, and chose a photo, and looked at the far end of the valley, and behind it take an army to walk in a monotonous and one movement regularly until it became a whole army, as if they were built together, one of the soldiers nose strap his shoes, imagine about the world to see him, and during this a small bright green color came up to him (lizard), I took a sound like wheezing, connect the soldiers to him boots and said reality to play around, but (the lizard) I took that high-pitched annoying sound, he looked at the soldier, walked up to her and smiled and completed his path, but she followed him, then he looked back again and found that there is more than one of them, they make a noise that stands right next to him and tells him:

- Go back to your herd, they shout to you.

He continued on his way, but she did not stop jumping next to him, followed him, and the stopped soldier fell on another, and there he said to him:

- Do you want to go with me?

The orchid's time from the jump, emitted by the voice of a rude soldier, which means Yes, then turning on his knees to join her red eyes, and that was a big mistake ..

Yes, the mistake cost him his life.

To pet her on the head like a pet, and not notice how she bared her sharp teeth, and tumbled back and jumped to offer her nose !! He sat and was distracted from the severity of the pain, and you were already taking a break from the lizards, and this lasted only a few seconds, until it turned into a structure without flesh and fat, and more and more of them crawled out of each hole of the terrier !! And even more!! Attacked the army of darkness from all sides and from all sides, and soared on the stock exchange, and did not stop

New structures were added to the overall structure of the terrible reality.

Or valley structures.

* * *

Sat (nightclub) next to (employees) to watch closely as (catfish model) takes the king away, as if he wants to say no to an important topic called (Lily's) dimension when a few of them approach hear him say no, and he raises his eyebrows:

- eh? sir, you trust this girl

The king smiled and continued:

- Why this question?

I didn't argue about the dossier, but he said as if he hadn't heard:

"You know that any catastrophe in the universe must be left behind by women.

- Sweetheart (catfish style) no need for pessimism.

- But Sir, this is ... ----

"You don't need to talk about it anymore.

The king was silent for a moment, and then added:

- I like to wake up your thoughts, the female half of the Universe, behind every great woman is the greatest of them, if not for the presence of a woman who was never born such a great life, and you exist in this life.

Then he left the king and returned to stand by the (staff) of the story of his owner asks himself:

"What made the king believe in this girl so quickly?

I didn't know that there is something third between the king and Lily that grows with every minute between them.

And he knows that when there is this thing, it melts at every border, and I am not the greatest of the great willingly.

* * *

The king put his hand on (Lily's) shoulder, why bother him or move a finger, as if she did not feel it, and said:

- (Lily) ..

I paid attention to him and looked melancholy at the whole world in her eyes:

- Are you here?

- I know the reason for this sadness in your eyes.

I tried to smile with a fake smile and exclaimed:

- True !!

- You do not trust me?

Get away from him and return her to him, she said to her slave:

- I did not mean it when I spoke.

Kill the file and said quietly:

- You don't have it.

Hania fell silent, and then added:

- I know that you lost your brother and uncle sadly, but God sent us to be with you in these minutes.

She turned to him to bring in his eyes, and on his face ECAA and she says:

- I do not understand what do you mean?

The King says stutters and his heart is beating wildly between his ribs:

- I just want to say that we will see you on Friday and we will look for your uncle and brother, no matter what ..

- But now it is difficult, especially since you are now a sick person.

- Didn't you say that you will regain your strength after this day?

- Yes.

- So there is always hope.

Her heart was beating somewhere between her ribs, as if he was beating only to hear this sound (wisely)

- He whispered and looked at his fresh smile, flashing in a distant world .:

"But it will make you late for your business activities.

- No, no, no ... never ... there is no delay.

She (Lily) watched it melt, like a piece of sugar in a cup of tea between King Genappa, taking it in silence and following her gaze, I suddenly heard a clang (catfish style), he jogged, and exclaimed that his breath gets from hyperbole:

- Sir, Sir.

He said the concern he raises his eyebrows:

- And what's in there?

- He dissapeared ..

The King's eyes widened as he quickly exclaimed:

- What's the point disappeared? And where did they disappear to?

She (Lily):

Let him come and he went this way or that.

He shook his head to say:

- I have never looked everywhere, and have not found any traces.

And so the Tsar, hearing this speech, even flushed, ran to the place where his master was lying before he disappeared, and after a few seconds, exclaimed (addressing Lily):

- Look !!

Because of Monday, to suggest where he found the tracks, I feel like the king said quickly as he looked to the East:

- It seems that the authors did not go by his choice, but carried something that left traces on the ground.

They considered everyone's silence as their king and led by one question:

- See what campaign (strand) is provided by launching without sound, leaving behind only its effects?

The answer was God knows what.

* * *

Seid hummed between the Southern kingdom of darkness, and took small creatures who were expecting an attack on you from all sides, the university seemed to be endless, and they ruined the meat, but they stopped and took the cries of pain, taught in the process, I took the blood coming from the bodies of non -stop, stopped the tiger and (CEO) and (Cohen).) In the rear, I could not believe this terrible scene, and everywhere women, screams of agony loudly pierced her ears, and then the queen interrupted the revolution, when the iron trembled and her gaze for several seconds clouded over, as if they did not feel what was happening around her, and heavy, terrible seconds passed, and the soldiers fell like flies in continuation, and suddenly raised her scepter to the sky, and the sky was rapidly thickening with dark clouds overhead. , Taking lightning appears between now and then !!! And so she said in a harsh voice and raised her hands to the sky, taking the head flying behind her in a wonderful landscape:

- The right of the king and the kingdom, and the creation of life and death, answer me, heaven, and the right to charm (even) terrible, get these waves of evil for my army.

- I shouted, blocking the roar of the sky.

- Get lalalalalalalalalalalalalala.

And so their conflict ended, so I took these animals, returned to hit the rock of reality, as if there were thin hands carrying it to the top of the highest rock !!! Thus, the business of animals, consisting of a number of their non-stop, continues, but there is something invisible that prevents their access to soldiers, the reputation of (CEO) and (Cohen) in the consciousness of their royal voice

He says that after he pacified the revolution:

"Leave the injured and release the tiger from Death Valley as quickly as you can.

Exclaimed (CEO) In Anger:

- Like this?

I interrupted his king explicitly this time, in a backward voice, and she, looking at him with flame, barely pierced the armor of his chest:

"Do not forget your position, captain, and do as you are told and do not need the intensity of the conversation.

You seized (Iran) the opportunity to prove to the Queen blind obedience to Him and rudely said to your masters:

"Do as you are told, captain.

First, look at him in silence, and if I have the opportunity to ask his neck with his sword, and since he is offended at him, offended at his disgusting and disgusting appearance, he knows that there is something between him and the Queen, but he is nothing cannot say, he smiled with the corner of his lips in a grin and said:

- Yes, ma'am.

It was the kindness of nature, but it will never change his fate, he was born in the kingdom of darkness and was chosen by the Queen as one of her squires, it is for the strength of his devotion, and when he spoke, the queen refused to obey him in order to remember what I did with her after long deliberations, interrupted by the Queen .:

- What are you thinking, why didn't you believe it now?

The (SEO) when I say the Queen said the word intermittent:

"Never, sir, nothing.

Then the concrete charred remains were lost in the sea of sad memories, and he shouted and took the sorrow of the bag and showed on his face his coarse army, shouting to the left:

- Come on, guys, back, quickly climb into the ranks, take weapons and clear your way, and do not stop and ... ---------

After a little silence and feeling that he was being torn to pieces, he (Cohen) smiled yellow like the smile of a demon, please enjoy his eyes when he felt the agony of his owner, and the wolves quietly told her:

- Why did you stop, commander, follow the order.

Look, no (CEO) is considered a motorcycle, and if I almost choked, then his heart was dead, and pressed on his teeth, and the temperature rose, and his eyes rose, but he gained strength and courage, he said, looking ahead and watching the rotation of the iron, which began to move, and could feel that the dog was heavy, like a mountain High .:

- Leave the wounded, there is no need to burden yourself with them.

All the wounded soldiers and others were laughing! And while doing it, some of them walked to the wounded in silence with tears in the eyes of the wounded, as if begging them not to leave them in this terrible place, and discussed bodies, and raised hearts, and grabbed one by the other, bass, desperately trying not leave them, and other of the wounded tried to get up; so do not stay in this place, but the pain was stronger than them, they fell to the ground a second time, and seconds of heavy and slow movement passed, everyone speaks in the silence of surprise filled with terrible sadness to their colleagues, and frankly, some areas must be:

- No Transamerica ..

And reluctantly, I ran over the foot of the page-turned-heart and prepared for the journey, leaving behind my wounded, most in need of help, to my terrible fate in the valley of buildings, and moving away from them to stop the magical attack of the little monster on the wounded, raised conflict and began to hesitate every fact without stopping.

These screams conveyed to me all my agony.
This is inside the cage a big (burgundy) scene is a grip on the rods of the cage, the dog should be dancing in his eyes tears, grief at the soldiers and their fate is sad, they took they smile ..

They seem to want ...

They seem to want ...

Until they disappeared over the horizon, leaving behind them once their masters, who became the prey of these little monsters ..

Yes, monsters have no heart

Deadly monsters.

* * *

Opening (a strand of) eyes in difficulty, Warsaw discussed the vision that had opened before him, and over time all this began to manifest itself and gradually, he found himself in the middle of the ruins of a city of deserted and strange architecture, among the trees, and imagined these ruins as wondrous, dotted here and there, like as if there was someone who distributed them evenly over time, it seemed that the trees were perennial so that the sun's rays could not afford to give them, and reach the Earth, and the climbing plants in large domes and marble columns in the eternal struggle for that, to reach the sunlight, and then he asked himself:

- See where I am? And what is this civilization? And where did the people of this city leave him?

Feeling that his body was numb, unable to move it, waiting a little to see what was around him and his thoughts, and tried to move forward, but failed, and at this time not because the body was under the influence of drugs; rather, because he was found tied up in the rocks.

This was no surprise !! Try to get rid of it, but it was limited in a controlled way, working for the file (wise) but not responsive, then the owner of the club but also not responsive, and repeated the call several times, but not responsive, no voice, intolerance, and split and his face, and tried several times to get rid of the restrictions, but not useful, and in close proximity to see him looks at his face with a hairy tail, brown eyes, fangs and a snub nose, and look at him until he cried out (strand) omnipotent, even almost ripped my throat ...

His cry narrowed in these thick and dark forests.

* * *

I knelt on the ground and, taking a system of checking these effects scattered here and there, then put my fingertips in some, after a period of silence twice in eternity ... stopping and hitting in each other's footsteps, he confidently said that in his eyes have charm:

- These effects are still hot.

- She exclaimed (Lily) quickly .:

"That means the kidnappers were here quite recently.

King continued the trend of effects with his own eyes and added:

- It is clear that the owners of these effects were not people at all.

- What do you mean, sir?

Therefore, he asked the owner and he answered the king:

- I mean that the owners of such effects are huge groups of monkeys.

- Lily whispered quickly .:

- You know .

The watcher (the summing model) flew into a rage, and then adjusted his gaze to the king and asked him:

-What now, sir?

- This means that we will get (strand) of these animals, at any cost.

"So you don't have to waste our time.

The three of us went among the trees, then they climbed far up a high mountain, they took wraps around the front spiral, and settled at the bottom of a small river, being at an alarming pace, and over time he took this road, rising, adding them a little so I asked (Lily) and Mai started to fall apart as I walked this road .:

- Where to go and started adding them whenever we go?

Here he said, trying to calm her down:

- Do not look down, but return to the rocks, and with caution.

I did what he asked the king, but she forgot that he wasn't looking down, and some small stones splintered from under her feet, and very quickly wanted to go to the bottom to cover my eyes, and beat her heart between her ribs in concern , and took the women playing with a lock of her hair, took the stones back from the intensity of the fear, I took moving steps, and (catfish style), and did not notice the beauty of this area, thus vulnerable, rising, which formed under his feet and the falling part them, and if she (Lily) we even have worn out the most, and put (catfish style) He stepped on her with his foot, and she felt stones the size of his huge, even quickly wore out and fell along with her master, and cried out (Lily) and quickly refused to give a quick reaction to his palm, I took the baton of stones that are falling down in confusion, and held on to him tighter, the road was narrow, so much so that the king could not do anything about it, and he was helpless scared, but he grabbed her and quietly told her:

- Grab him and don't let him score, please.

She felt that her heart would tell about the horror, and tried to cleave to it yet, but it was too heavy, so much that she began to ache and tears out of her eyes, and a moment of difficult eternity passed, and she wanted for a moment if forcefully with ten men to drag him upstairs, here the faded eyes and saw his eyes, as if looking at them for the first time, and tried to take them in her palm, but his fingers little by little slipped away from her, but her tears were warmed by the increased diameter of the throne, and shook from within her, like a chicken that fell into a puddle of water on a cold winter night, and she saw these tears, a smile rose on her face (catfish style), whispering to him ::

- Don't try anymore .. it's time for the team.

I tried to use his grip, but he very quickly fell with his heavy weight to the bottom, and it was all a continuation of the date .:

- For Bea ..

Taking a body (catfish style) pretends to be

Objectives

Non-stop ... to an unknown fate that God knows.

* * *

Unless the disk of the sun gave me the history of a minimum of darkness and took it, hiding among the palm trees, I took the birds back to their nests to clear the sun from the New World, this disk turned pale to see how this exotic gallops on the ground with prey, as if in haste, up these sandy hills, that from other hills, and after a period of ups and downs and in the valleys between taller plants and rocks hiding everywhere, attract the horse's bridle, firmly stop again, leaving a thick trail of dust around you, and enroll in the said alien detachment .:

- Expect (fear) let's rest here tonight.

Taking a horse, neighing, as if understanding the words of the knight, he took as a basis the Earthen front part, which fell on the knight's back and, grabbing some things, put it on the ground, then tied it to one of the stones and went to collect firewood to cover them .

He sat down, lit a fire and, according to the accumulated discharge, took out a map from the folds of his clothes, said aloud, as if talking to someone next to him:

- Where to go with him, (A.J.) is there?

Take a close look, and then point your finger at the point where we need, and exclaim:

- So now I want to get to this place and as soon as possible.

Then he added, folding the map and looking at the stars:

- It seems that the time has come, and we will soon see what we have long hoped for.

The silence again made him swallow saliva, and in an even fuller demonic tone, the genie emerged from hell .:

- And then I will be the last thing that awaits everyone.

Then he laughed a terrible and terrible laugh as much as possible and exclaimed:

I will be the worst of their worst nightmares.

Taking a laugh

Laughs nonstop.

* * *

Stop the revolution of the iron queen, darkness, and stop behind her, the tiger of the mountain range, namely in the voice of an irritated, and across the entire top of the garden I hear her voice ::

"We will set up camp here tonight," he ordered.

Following the women's movement, I move the file behind her, and fly away from the back of the bull, and land on the ground, and she holds the wand, a miracle, and takes a step to the side while pointing (CEO) at the army that camped here for the night and feels the fire , and then Monday lands, and Cohen quickly goes to his queen and tries to kill her, the owner is already caring for the great's cage, and our companions, and the dog, and then he picks up and shakes his tail, and (Burgundy) is available and refers so that makes the eyes silent. as if something was happening between them, or as if he wanted (CEO) to say something closer and hit the bars of the cage with his fist, and looked at each other, then decided to smile in the silence of the story of his embarrassed master and disappeared among the soldiers, saying: that it moves backward (burgundy):

- What's the matter, son?
He replied shaking his head:

"I don't know, uncle, but there is something strange about this Captain, as if he had come to visit us, and I realized that he was going to tell me something; he read it in his eyes, but for some reason hesitated. we left and returned among the soldiers ..

He paused for a while, and then, changing his gaze, continued:

- From his look it is clear that this leader does not face the dry severity invisible behind these features, which no one knows.

- I understand your point of view, son.

Suddenly he turned to this thing, changed his tone to a tone of enthusiasm, and yelped as if he had discovered something he did not know:

"Listen, uncle, I won't lock us here for long.

You saw the edges of this thing, when he heard it, he raised an eyebrow and asked impatiently:

- Like this?

He said not in a whisper:

- I will break this lock and aim at the soldiers in the middle of the night.

-Can you really pull it off?

"Yes, uncle, I can, if God pleases, but I hope midnight comes quickly.

He called the thing of his master and wished to succeed (Burgundy) in his plan, and that they would break out of this Great cage no matter what the cost, even if at the cost --------

His life.

* * *

And what he saw (strand) This torment - her red eyes, brown hair thick on the periphery of his vision, even cut his heart in horror, as if an electric shock had struck him, and he cried out from the surprise of the injury, and did not believe his eyes, and was surprised About myself:

- Where was this gorilla so huge and terrible ?!

"It must be a nightmare.

And then he closed his eyes tightly, maybe he woke up from this, and after a few seconds he opened them, and the picture around him changed, his still red eyes silently looked at the wondrous, like a group of statues that took possession of the sculptor to sculpt him, for in ugliness and horror reigns in the atmosphere, for these faces with sharp fangs and oil falling from them, and what kind of noses, snub-nosed monkeys, and here he knew that he was living with the terrifying reality of the inevitable, and his escape was limited.

And in order to surrender and stop my movements and screams, until I accepted this huge animal roar and scream in annoying voices, and the delivery, some of them squeezing the stone with small blows on the stone with the largest ones, the scene was terrible and incomprehensible for Max, and his owner from the inside when he learned that death is inevitably coming between the fangs of these fierce creatures, and suddenly heard a sound like a scream saying:

"Stop it, children, stay away from the sacrifice.
And so that I could hear these beasts making noise, until everything suddenly calmed down, and the silence of the meeting moved aside in the course of it, so that he took the search system for the source of the sound, until he saw an old hag emerging from one of the destroyed mansions, they used on a stick the proven human skull of a small child, I took the approaching sea and behind it, gray and gloomy, smelly, dirty, and above her hair sat a piece of canvas, pierced by rats in every place, but there were tufts of her white hair, which can be seen from its outer mind that he had not washed for many years, came closer to him and looked at him with a face that simulates the presence of a problem with a dead bee, and she smiled so that her teeth were broken or what was left of them, she said high voice:

- Do not be afraid, Mister Time, you are in good hands.

I looked at her with horrifying apprehension from the organization of a disgusting and repulsive smell, which is similar to the smell of decaying bodies:

- Who are you? Why did you bring me here? And why did you tie me up like that, but I did nothing to you? What is the secret of these shortcomings? And why am I here -----------

I interrupted him with a laugh similar to that of Satan's mother, and said:

- Our guest seems to have a lot of questions.

Then she suddenly stopped laughing, and her features were the devil himself, she had bloodshot eyes, and she went up to him, even smelling the mold in her mouth, and she says:

"Here, in the land of the lost, you have never entered a person and never.

Then she smiled and with laughter became hysterical, and her nerves tensed (a strand), and the blood rushed to the brain for herself, and he found himself screaming strongly and strongly, as if he had never been captivated:

- Enough, enough.

The old man's silence and keen gaze widened her eyes as he threw fear at the most powerful of the titans, making him hesitate to say:

- I didn't mean ... didn't mean to bother you, but ... ---

He swallowed with difficulty, trying to control himself, with his fear and horror, and asked:

- Why am I here?

Didn't his experiments get old, but she looked at him for a long time, then turned her back on him and left him in confusion, then she said, looking at him out of the corner of her eye:

"Today is the century of our existence here, and in every memory, which should not be a victim, but our ritual.

After a pause for a while, and then stepping on a stone that came out of her part in the shape of a tongue, she stood on the edge and raised her hands to the top, the littered area behind her was a magnificent sight, she said in a high-pitched voice like a cry:

"This sacrifice must be human.

Shuttlecock (strand) and stop his heart when he said:

- I have the honor to sacrifice myself to our solemn anniversary.

I took the victim and the gorilla with a cry and stones, which tried to free itself from its chains, but it did not work, and not rushing to go as quickly as if the floor agreed to put an end to it.

End as a sacrifice to a human group of specialized animals.

* * *

The King (Lily) struck tears falling from her eyes like lava lane released from an erupting volcano and through a wildly vibrating, and in her imagination, an image (catfish style) that falls to the bottom, and words of regret and:

- I lost it ..

He said::

"You did your best, but it was harder than rejecting him.

- I never let go of my hand, maybe if I hold on to it more, you can work.

- No, honey, it will help in any case ... God is the one who wrote that this is the end, no, it is not in our hands to change at the command of God.

There was something in her eyes that he said in a whisper:

- I must now control myself and be our way, otherwise we will catch up with him at the same factory.

Then he puts his fingertips to her tears and says:

"I don't want those blue eyes hiding behind a stream of tears, please.

She shook her head affirmatively, and he, leaving them, walked in front of her and said:

- Let's go and complete our mission, the fate of the whole world is now connected with us.

Feeling her footsteps, she followed him and tried to remove the image (catfish style) from her eyes, sinking down, and a minute of solemn silence passed, suddenly interrupted by the road, and the stopped file system above said:

- Looks like it's registry time, can you registry up?

- Yes I can .

We take a salted stone, climb, and she follows him, and during her they say:

- Don't look down, whatever the motivation for it.

After some time of shopping, the silent King said:

- It seems that the end has come at last.

Indeed, the king climbed up and followed Lily to the end, but was amazed at something located below, after which he considered the reaction normally, and what to do until she saw the organization of the earth, which is very far away at this height of the high-rise, even a dart at a minimum in the next seconds, she felt that a black cloud appeared, creeping up to her eyes and head, and stopped time for him, suddenly found herself free in the air, left stones at the bottom of her body below, and did not realize what was happening, and then suddenly she remembered one thing , hesitated before her, namely:

An image (catfish style) that falls to the bottom quickly awesome ..

Shake without stopping.

* * *

The Queen of Darkness sat on this large stone, and she returned her to her camp, as if she wanted to separate from everyone, silence enveloped the place around her, and from afar ... Yazbek approached her, and his heart beat faster. with force between his ribs, as if he feared something would happen. That, or that he was about to do something that pushed him into this confusing situation, he stopped next to her and hesitantly faked a smile on his lips, a smile like that of an evil snake, before injecting poison into his victim to paralyze her heart muscles and let her slowly die, then he said in a voice full of uncertainty, and all of his cells flinched:

My lady - Don't you want me ... tonight ... Huh?

She did not speak and did not pay attention to him, but was silent, as if she had not heard anything from his speech, and here our friend felt that the blood was rushing to his head more than dark, and that his temperature had risen to indicates that he held out his palm to wipe off the beads of sweat that had accumulated on his broad forehead, and took two steps towards the Imam, fearless and indecisive, as if he was afraid of this progress or understood that his queen did not want him to exist, but was imposed on her, perhaps she give in to him and agree with his idea of how insane he is with his endless evil ideas and his voice dressed in indecision, as if he were a little child learning to speak:

Mon - la - TN -

She interrupted him, saying in a voice that seemed to come from the depths of a deep well:

Go away, idiot, this is not your time, go ... you don't belong here.

He knew the meaning of these words well, but did not move, but continued his strange and unnecessary insistence:

But oh-oh-oh-mall-

She quickly turned to him, her eyes widening strangely, causing both fear and horror, and said to him with obvious disgust, as if she hated him:

Looks like you lost your hearing, I told you to leave, you bastard rat. And he saw her eyes, even he knew that he might have to leave and quickly, until he lost everything, and then collect the fragments left after this fear that tormented his body quickly, because of the gaze of his fiery queen, eerie, definitely, and then trot away from her and leave her in her evil and knows what he is doing there in her silence, and knows that in her silence she is doing something that he cannot bear in front of him, that something extremely evil ..

Something black.

Or explained that they bring something with dark magic, but the question here didn't get it ?!

The answer was as terrible as possible.

* * *

And the owls flew in the sky to look for food for themselves, working tirelessly and not getting bored, as if she boasted that she was the only bird that robbed in the evening at night, and below the army of the queen of darkness was standing, continuing her camp, it was quiet here, except that you could hear faint whispers coming from somewhere nearby, and if we hinted at our opinion a little, then the creature whispered with (tan) in the faintest light. :

- What are you, son?

The look of wine about this seemed to be afraid to hear one of the soldiers, and then answered in a low voice that intensified the beating of his heart, so that he felt that the sound of these blows would be heard by the inhabitants of heaven:

"I'll pick this lock, sir, and we'll be free tonight.

The silence will swallow his saliva, and then, perhaps, he will see one of the soldiers that he had, and again whisper, clutching his fist at the greatness of the great. :

"I have brought something that will break this castle of the valley structures, and then we will take care of the dead of this night and the approaches of this army of the damned and their madmen.

Then I feel like a thing, seeping into the folds of his heart, says that fear has taken a large sum from him:

- Be careful, son, don't make a fuss if we get caught. God knows how our fate will turn out then.

He did not talk to the owner and did not say anything, except that the dog perceives sounds more like a whistle, he (Tan) told you:

"Enjoy some quiet dude and don't make a sound or they'll find us and we'll get out of here soon, so take your time ..

The dog lay silently on the floor, as if he understood what his friend had said, decided to voice it, and then left his wine and went to the door of the cage, and looked to lock it on the lion's face and the keyhole in his mouth, and already realized that his fangs are sharp, and then he said, looking at him in surprise:

What a fantastic castle shape !! He must have made you a professional artist or a demon, he wanted to strike terror into Zee's heart and ---

He was interrupted by a thing, saying that she squeezes his shoulder from behind:

- Son do not waste time, broke him before one of the soldiers felt us.

And then she said these simple words, so he felt that someone was moving around to let in the weakest, which was pressing on the shoulder of wine:

- Shut up, son ... it seems that someone is awake there; because I can feel it and hear the voice of grasses moving under the weight of his legs.

The look (burgundy) even hints at this person, and indeed the look, and he moved away from them, he gave them back and said to people::

- This is one of the soldiers. he seems to have left the bedroom to relieve himself.

Then he continued his words saying:

"Then stop and wait until he goes to bed and falls asleep.

Minutes passed ... and a difficult eternity dragged on, and after a long silence a thing whispered:

"I think the time has come, boy, to trust God and do what you think.

He moved away (Burgundy) and grabbed the lock, and his heart beat madly, so much so that I feel that his heart is about to jump out from under his ribs, then he lifted a bone so that it fell on this lock surprisingly enough, something happened there , which I did not expect, I came to life and quickly, as if by devilish magic !! Then he bit off his fingers and took the burgundy, yelling and yelling incessantly.

And crying (Burgundy), and the hot blood of his fingers, and the bone fell out of his hand, and he does not realize what happened ?! And the soldiers woke up, took the word they must have, and in the distance everyone heard the sound of the laughter of the queen of darkness and took away the Echo that had left her.

And hesitates

Endless.

* * *

Having offered the gorillas huge (strands) and his limitations, he said that his difficulties are trying to get rid of them, horror appeared in his eyes, and took every ounce of it out of fear, and he screams, saying them strongly:

- You are a monster, you bastards ...

But what of the answering cries, and here this old man exiled to them is her figure of a terrible exile, a path to a giant rock, and stands in front of her awaiting her orders, she said to them with her sharp high voice, which resembles the meow of cats:

- Quickly ... tie his legs and send him upstairs.

These animals, already old, quickly carried them out, and found their master head down and feet up, turning his head straight to where the nozzle was, the hole from time immemorial did not show its end, the light disappeared into the darkness of his heart, distant and in the form of a theater .. she raised the old man's hands up and chose a place behind her, and from behind she took the rest of her teeth, which were black and indicated a lack of hygiene and negligence:

- You are the Gods .. Accept simple happiness and prosperity from this sacrifice, with our experienced team.

And that the reputation of the owner of these words, even of the rebellion of its members, knew that the end would come in that well of darkness, taking on attempts to escape from them, and at the same time he wanted to show something supernatural that gave this plant a frightening look, and save him from these terrible animals, this old man is terrible, shouted at the top of his voice:

- Help! - - - help! - - - help!

But the old man screamed in a harsh annoying voice to the maximum extent, she uttered a victory cry, and began to growl as gorillas, exposing her fangs and drooling, and lay on the ground in the form of savages, in the office there was a screaming terrible and incomprehensible to Max, and the old man at the top of the cliff took the sea and flew after her in the mythical scene, raising his hands to the sky, accepting the question, which sounded scary and depressing, as a prelude to the future.

* * *

At that moment I found (Lily) myself in the air, and in a matter of seconds after that, twice all my life in front of her suddenly, and found her body tumbling to the bottom like a rock fall from the top of a mountain, and felt a moment of utter horror and fear, I made an attempt to achieve something, but, unfortunately, there was nothing to relate to, and she felt that the world around her had disappeared, and lost the sense of time and place, and suddenly the flight time landed, I looked up into her eyes and looked at the folder, grandma grabbed her hand and she makes sure that he saved her from this fate !! ...

Dana, she raised her face to me with a thin smile and said in a voice full of love and tenderness and longing:

- Do you want to leave without saying goodbye to me?

Then he added that he abandons her to the very top, his eyes never leave her eyes, he took his heart to be in love with her, she also swirled in the sea of his eyes and soared into his heavens, and is reflected in the fact that he has :

- Hold on to me.

She lifted the file in her hand, stepped back from the edge and looked at the place of her fall, and saw the ground very far away, sent a sigh of relief and said that she had no evidence that she had survived such a terrible fall:

I thought I would die inevitably.

Then the king tried to say something, but I interrupted him with an exclamation of greeting and raised my head up:

- Stop words.

The silence of the king took over and what he saw surprised! - Not knowing what is happening ?! she whispered and turned her head as if she had heard something coming from afar. :

- I hear a sound (strand) !! ...

Listen, the king is walking through the air, and then he exclaimed, hearing the master's voice, called to him from behind the folds of the air:

- Yes, I can hear it too .. but it is mixed between many voices, as far as I can tell.

"But I can hear him clearly ... and I know he's there.

"No wonder you have the advantage of the strange and the surprising.

"Forget it now and don't have to waste a lot of time, it looks like its owner is in trouble and we need to rescue him as soon as possible.

- Can you identify the source of the sound?

- Yes, I can determine the source of his good.

She pointed north .. she said earlier to hurry on her way and behind her:

- Go here .

The Queen and Lily marched quickly, even arrived in an area with wooded trees and tangled branches, thick leaves, as in their footsteps, even taking the sound slowly and clearly, and then the king said:

- The limit of your movement; and not to detect it.

Then we will rise on Monday into the silence of the tiger, which lies in wait for prey in the blink of an eye, and if we need two more so that we can see more clearly, we will observe what is happening with their master ... and then in a whisper we will call the king:

"It looks like the old man is their leader, and they move on their own.

I asked him if the scene followed from her place:

- Do you have any plan?

"I'm going to attack them, and she will call me, then you must get rid of the master from his chains and run as quickly as possible.

See to add a look to his facial features in earnest:

- The concept is ..

I looked at him and said No, she is pure in his eyes, she has a heart and his love between the ribs:

- And you what do you do?

- And I will run too, it is important for the two of you to be saved at any cost.

Be quiet a little, he said, whispering to her and wanting that moment, if time is available to them, when this limit:

- And if I can't escape? you should know that this will be our last goodbye.

Leaving no way to say or comment, he left her and disappeared among the trees with extreme speed, and she felt that her heart was torn and splattered, or he got up from his place and walked with the king among the trees, stayed for a second look at the place where he needs to before he leaves her in silence, but she heard the old man's cry, looked at the stage in front of her and averted her eyes; The king jumped between the gorillas, heading towards (the strand), and to see his old man, even shouted, referring to the broken back teeth:

- Kill him ... don't let him sacrifice himself even at the expense of your bodies.

The gorilla of all went into the corner, heading towards the king with the greatest fury and ferocity, opening the jamb farther from the place of its owner, right here to collect (Lily) himself back in order, not forgetting to say that the owner quickly went to untie (the strand), and he caught a glimpse of her next to him .. even the uncertified ones chanted:

- Finally you came .. I thought I would die inevitably.
She said no and gasped. :

- No need to chat and waste time, there are yours away from the wellhead, so that I can catch you decipher the chords.

And quickly did what she said, and untied him, and gave him his weapon, which she carried on her back ... and exclaimed::

"I think you're celebrating your health and wellness right now, it looks like my magic cure has returned quickly."

- Yes, let's return it to God, so that later he can heal you with magic.

"Therefore, fight with the utmost ferocity, otherwise you will die as soon as possible between the jaws of these disgusting creatures, and enchantments and magic medicine will no longer help here.

Then I noticed the gorilla, what happens when the Holy Well, the migration of their second group of gorillas are available, the decryption file is the fastest of them, he grabbed the old one, which took a cry and a cry, but he took her hand well and tried to push her towards him, saying ::

"I don't need to scream anymore, witch, it's time for you to leave this world.

But what happened was a miracle for all the laws of nature, it carried in itself the activity of an old man, how early youth gains its youth !! Coming out of safety, she found herself between the folds of her dress, tore her skinny body out of the king's embrace and accepted Bentsen's fight with cruelty, ferocity, and then uttered in her sharp and high voice the ghostly ironic smile that had already appeared on her face:

"I don't think you can reach me that easily.

The answer file is exported impressed with their swiftness and determination to commit suicide:

- And what prevents me from achieving this goal? there is?

The cunning and ingenuity and dexterity of the riders threw the old man to the ground and began to laugh, so that I feel like a king, that he misses the smell of her bad breath, then she continued her words and said:

"The Force had to die, mortal ..

Then he carried his body upstairs and then returned to fight fiercely from the beginning, he asked himself, puzzled:

- Where did she get this old man's strength in this youth ?!

During this conflict is unique .. Chance's file drowned his gun in her chest and freed her eyes, and screamed with a terrible cry, and opened her mouth from the severity of the damage done, and quickly took his weapon, and pushed it away from
him with his foot, and grabbed the old man , let go of her, and pulled the bloody stream of Fayyad from her fingers, and took a step back with slow and unsteady steps until he reached the edge of the well, and her gaze was fixed on the king, and all the anger and minimum appeared between them, and then he screamed loudly cry, which in the darkness of this well, well, choose something else under you, and disappear her voice forever in your lonely darkness, now and then look into the folder on it to find that the scene stopped around him in silence, where in time the gorilla will follow what is happening and lift a finger, but will notice her warm breath. As volcanoes from the realization of his smoke will come out of their noses, so they choose the old man, even twice for a few seconds, and one of the gorillas quickly screamed, as if she suddenly woke up from a coma, and then everyone went crazy, as if they got angry from - for the loss of their leader, and so they picked up speed and ran at him, but he did something impossible, he jumped acrobatically, settling himself between the spirits !! - The ribbons burst due to overload ... - exclaimed (Strand), smiling, placed his weapon in the neck of one of the gorillas, and then quickly disarmed it to protect:

- Welcome, Sir.

Dip three in the back and the file matches it:

"And this seems inevitable to us after they have surrounded us in this way.

With the tip of her eye, she found (Lilia) the entrance to one of the destroyed temples left behind, and behind it brave knights are fighting fast and fiercely:

- Let's step back to get me this rate, otherwise we will die.

- exclaimed Strand, who resolutely defends himself:

- It's a good idea.

Silence to say that one of the gorillas quickly followed in derision:

- Will you be with us if we go there ?!

- Let me leave first, and then be as it is; our situation here is very difficult.

Leading the three back to back carefully until they entered the temple and stopped the gorillas, but strong and ferocious wild beasts continued to advance with their attack on them, and in the center of the temple there was a large lake, at the bridge, divided into two halves, and next to with this bridge there was some kind of timber, and judging by the appearance of this cloak, it is very old and has not been used by anyone for any purpose for a long time.

When attacked by these gorillas, they are fierce and loud (to Lily):

- Come on, we'll cross the bridge .. nothing has changed.

And quickly all three found themselves in the middle of the bridge and suddenly they were stopped by (Strand) phone:

- One minute ... don't move !!

These words were like a hammer hitting them on the head in this wartime, this is the dossier that was in the article, and also the Case (Lily), and all where they saw (strand), and they found that the gorillas stopped far from the bridge, as if afraid to cross after them, and took the trail in silence, wonderful !! ..

Silence pushes terror to hearts.

The (Lily):

- It seems that something scares them, I feel it, but I don't know what exactly ?!

The surface of the pond was calm, but he suddenly became very worried and jumped out in a group of bubbles quickly to the surface, and in front of everyone's eyes, the vibration of its surface increased, and the bubbles began to grow more and more from the bottom to the surface, began to move from one place to another, until he got to the bridge, and then suddenly fell silent and seconds passed, every heart was pounding terribly, and suddenly (Lily) screamed with a loud cry that shook everything around. :

- To cross the bridge with arrows ... there is something under this pond.

Something terrible seemed from under the water, smashed the end of the bridge between its frightening jaws !!! Taking the spewing wood in every place, and taking it towards the world very quickly and smashing everything in its path, it seems like he carries with him the signature of the last thing - his staff .------

The signing of the terrible is inevitable ..

Yes that.

* * *

Next to the wheels of the large cage that was inside our companions, the Queen stood, looking at them in silent amazement, accepting the dogs that should have refused their presence in this place for some reason in the same, but she quickly looked at him, as if she understood what to say to them, she widened her eyes in a strange way, and there made a sound from the floor, seen through her in pain, then quickly retreated to the end of the cage, then shrank in some, it was clear that she took the silence and uttered whining, it was felt (burgundy) that was going to the phone, quickly addressed his conversation to her:

- Enough ..

She silently looked at him, whether horror was terrible in herself, in her master from the inside, as if I had hit a stone wall, but it was his courage, he became better on her tone:

"I haven't done anything to you. ..

His hair varies from the system to its depths, and they take his insides from the inside, they torment him, and heavy seconds go by forever, he does not know what is happening to him, but he is almost sure that they carry a lot of company between the folds of one and the same, and they can do a lot, and knows the limits of their evil, the only Almighty God, and during this I heard her voice inside my head saying to him:

- Don't try it again.

Her voice ceased, and then looked at his wounded palm and had to let her in easily, while the abduction of Burgundy took his palm away from her, raising one of her eyebrows, not even the ghost of an evil smile was in the corner of her mouth, and looked at that which was tainted with the blood of Burgundy, spoken by her voice this time and the smell of evil smells. :

- Is that your blood?

Here I feel (Burgundy) that the blood is rushing to his head, and he must speak and shout in her face and do whatever he wants, pull himself together and shout in her face:

Let's go alone ... let's go .. we haven't done anything to you .. we don't know what the reason was that kept us here ?!

I did not move, but silently looked at him, intensifying my coup. :

- Leave her alone.

Then they run to you with the bars of the cage with their fists, and they have to say something, but I feel that it is Haven to open his mouth, the thread of his mouth with a thread, I don't know where it came from ?! .. I took out his eyes and took his heart pounding so hard that it almost exploded between his ribs, taking on a muffled sound, shaking the bars of the cage and it changed his facial features in a strange way, I feel like a thing that something abnormal is happening, he raised his hand up, as if looking for his owner, exclaimed::

- This (wine) is going on, son ?!

This creature is silent, and tries to hear what is happening around him, but he is plotting something .. he said:

- Don't say anything, my son; and my heart is not safe.

She smiled the queen said For clarity:

- Why haven't you answered my question yet ?!

And this reputation is her voice, even in turn the rods of the cage to the owner, and in turn his body and face, until he got to his mouth, and he described this picture well to his mind, and then exclaimed in frustration::

- What did you do?!

She smiled even more at the irony of his look in my (burgundy) eyes, which she perceived in confusion and cream at the same time, then picked up and accepted what was hanging from his blood, and then said:

What a delicious taste!

The thing in her face exclaimed in the power of anger:

- I do not know what is the point of booking tickets, why all this torment?

I heard her say to him:

- The future tells you interest .. I will worry about your life, because they paid a lot on my way; to achieve what I am aiming for, I hope.

Now it remains to disappear among the tents, and the creature (burgundy) will be puzzled by its curiosity, and if it wants ... until the mouth returns to normal. it is a sigh of relief and exclamations of joy, as well as anger and fear:

What a wicked and damned woman!

- Exclaimed the subject, he almost smiles; because I feel like its owner bounced back and sat down patting on the back. :

"Don't talk too much, son; because the word at this time of judgment, the work of your paintings, I do not know what you can do with us, is it a woman ?!

The sigh calmed down a bit:

- Honestly, uncle.

And everyone is shocked ... and stop the dog behind (guilt) who took a look ahead and watched the sun rise from behind the trees in shame, how fear appears to come out of my darkness and its black shadow passed, with the hope that there will be a new day, brings with it a chance to break out of this cage, and this generation is terrible, and far you have taken the sunrise little by little.

* * *

In the middle of the desert, there is no end in sight, and this sun has settled in the big city with huge brown walls, huge towers, so that they reach the clouds. can you imagine what heads some have in it !! Arranged massive stone statues here and there, meaningfully, they seemed to have been carved by professional artists; he mastered everything and did not miss a single detail, while the statues look like gigantic creatures taking in between these towers in silence.

The man appeared in a strange shape, but this is not the strangest of his face, the color of flowers received horror in the heart of everyone who sees him for the first time, he had too long hair, glow under the heat of the sun, it seemed that it could burst into people from for the colors of his red-hot, then glancing forward through his organization of a loved one who was in possession, and a few seconds passed like lightning, and then took a clenched fist and said:

- To be honest, Mr. Minister, it seems to me that this generation does not intend to reward us.

I went up to the minister, there was a face that other features in different colors, the lower limit, wear less sharp in his strangeness too, and then said to him, surprised:

- What work, sir?

- I will not do anything .. we will wait until the danger arises.

Wait a bit and follow his words ... the weight was a platform to hear what he had to say, don't move very carefully, and then the king continued his words, looking ahead:

- And then the first will always be better.

The minister asked, he was surprised:

- What are you talking about, sir?! .. How can we resist such a large army ?! In particular, in the presence of these massive creatures is there ?! Oh sir, if we resisted. you will be lost - this is our destiny, and then we will tell everything, we thus brought us to our homes and our children, and God knows the end.

He looked at the king in anger and said in the package:

- Does it look like cavalry?

The Supreme Minister shook every atom of his body, shouted to the king, adding:

- Do you have cheese in their language?

Hair weight confusedly said the word intermittently:

Yes sir, I know ....

The King interrupted him, saying:

- For our army immediately; because she can attack them at any moment.

Then look up with your outstretched hand. The Army of Darkness said to B and about the wonderful words of a heavy man:

- And we will immediately deliver them to the danger zone and will not retreat for anything ...

The silence that should have followed the rest of the conversation:

"Or, whatever the consequences.

After this long conversation, it was so ... he is the master of this place.

The silence is frightening to the extreme.

* * *

Taking this wooden bridge turns into violence, removing our heroes very quickly, after which the experienced horror of this unknown frightens, and approaching them very scary, we almost got caught alone; but the king acted automatically, jumped high and then settled on the second, and followed her (Lily), but (Strand) was already three so he took the creature and the thing breaks the bridge furiously behind him to pay for services in each place, and two the eyes of the King and I (Lily) watched this scene terribly in horror, and walked through them very slowly, and lost all sense of what was happening around them.

And suddenly this creature (strand) ascended strongly swayed the ground beneath it to rise into the air, and he swung his arms and legs, as if floating in the air, and then very quickly went down, and at first glance it seemed that it would be in the water next with this object, but he fell from the jaws of this creature, which broke the last part in that wooden bridge with the utmost strength, and settled its owner on the shore, it is incredible that he survived, this is what this creature looks like in his head out of the water, and fell to unpack folder down, not believing what happened. He sees!! and gasped (Lily) in disarray !! And the heartbeats (strands) accelerated in horror !! I saw the largest crocodile you can imagine, it at first glance seems to be extinct from time immemorial prehistoric times ?! Looking at your master with eyes and a rumbling voice, stop in place, fix yourself as if on the basis of an attack, and (a strand) in its place he could not do anything, as the hypnotized one is absent in the world, it was proved that looking at the alligator's teeth sharply, and suddenly attacked you, I feel that death is going terribly between these teeth; but the king was furious and quickly pulled him away from him, and then shouted:

"Not for real this time ... come on, get up quickly and follow me. S (Strand) quickly regained consciousness, and went after the king, and followed his (Lily), and taking a creature without a gift, and it was in his head, is one thing ... Escape from the crocodile that follows them, they took a run over trees and rocks, and the real advance then run a second time, and took the line to do what they don't know, that maybe it's birds or animals, and they don't look after them, and their heart knocks heavily from the intensity of fear, and suddenly the king stopped them at the receiving end of his breath and behind him, but did not find the alligator, he stood for a moment as a silent Rose (strand) to the Earth from an overabundance of efforts in flight with his life. from the mouth of this creeping giant, (lily) I sat down on one of the stones, I can't believe that the teeth of this terrible creature survived, and then the king bowed, and he was breathing with difficulty and uttered the words intermittently:

"We're almost having lunch for this terrible creature.

She exclaimed (Lily) and said:

- The one who ratified.

Then I looked around to inspect the place, and found that they were inside, like a huge dome that fell from part of it to seep out of the star-shadow light of plants and plants equal to the open light, as if pushing to get the place .. proverb:

- Where are we? ... What kind of place is it?!

Look on Monday to ask her ... and he told (Strand) Linda about it and headed upstairs and then said:

- It looks like we are inside the dome of a Palace or a temple .-----

He showed the king to shut up ... Wang tried to say something, but he exclaimed, frowning:

- Stop the dog.

In the silence of everyone they hear, they can hear something, they noted that there is a thin voice, like sibilant leaves here and there, and take hesitation and feel free ..

This is becoming clearer and clearer.

And suddenly something happened to make everyone scream in horror !?

So what happened to them was terrible for maximum effect !! ...

* * *

(Jafar) undertook to plunder the land with his horse in order to plunder, and reached a wide land surrounded by hills on each side, and as soon as he reached it ... he stopped his horse and got off it, and he looked at this valley imprisoned between hills, and black evil appeared in his eyes, then he said to himself Spitefully about the demons:

What a suitable valley for my next surprise.

Then he added, looking around, with a smile on his lips filled with the ugliness of the whole world:

A: It will be the greatest surprise to those who come after me, it will have one signature ... the signature that everyone knows and fears him the most.

He left the horse, threw off the scarf from his shoulders and looked at the clear sky, and then he raised his hands to him, and then his eyes took on a strange shape, the black spot disappeared, and his eyes became completely white, and he muttered strange, incomprehensible words and began to intensify his voice, and the horse began to jump. In its place there was a light breeze, her screeching intensified, her voice became louder and her tone faster, and with it the air blew sharply and the sky thundered, and the sun quickly disappeared, replacing it with gloomy black clouds, and the same with dry grasses, who began to fly here and there without stopping, and he stood motionless and did not vibrate ... ... despite the fact that his clothes flew and the sand interfered in his face, as if something made him stand firmly on earth, and the earth began to tremble as he intensified stronger than his words, and suddenly he calmed down Everything fell on his face ...

The seconds passed very slowly, then the water began to quietly come out of the ground, and so he stood looking at her in silence and smiling maliciously and with satisfaction, and the stream of water began to increase, as if it were an eye and opened. without stopping, and the valley quickly filled up and he climbed one of the hills and began to follow the stage, and it was swollen. He took a small octopus out of his bag, which was inside a glass bottle, and then he took it and watched as he moved his eight hands in the palm of his hand, and no one knew what was going on in his head at that time, and calmly bowed at the rim water and left him to dive. Then he started laughing as he rode his goddess to disappear, and as soon as he disappeared ... until the page of water trembled, a group of bubbles appeared on the surface, and then they began to grow and expand as if the water was erupting, and all of a sudden everything calmed down and the page of water returned to rest, the clouds passed and the sun came out of New York to cast its golden rays on this quiet lake, which had recently been a dry valley full of stones and sand.

Before examining the file, what happened ?! .. These creatures sit on their faces, and their bodies are strong and; for this reason, I did not see someone to the fact that these creatures, it could be a swarm of bats that inhabit this dome, were annoyed by their entrance into it, taking each one holding his face with his hands, but the circulation of these creatures, heavy sounds and disturbing, like a nightmarish horror, while the clumping of these creatures hair (Lily) .. which I took on a journey and try to get rid of them, or (strand) so he took a fall and links waving his arms and on his face, but he stumbled about something and fell into a pit, missed seconds of sight, and accidentally signed (Lily) in the same place, but the king grabbed him at the last moment, but these little creatures continued to attack his face, and suddenly Monday fell and missed in the dark, taking a fall without stopping and I took (Lily) scream and scream

And the kitchen, she thought the end was already here. moment, and know that the future does not matter anymore.

* * *

Sheikh (Abdullah's) panic attacks, suddenly, as if he had been electrocuted, trigger the frightened holding shoulder (burgundy) and clench it with a fist:

- It seems that the sky is overcast ... there will be thunder and lightning and Seoul is red.

He looked (tan) from the bars of the cage at the sky and was taken aback by the conversation about what he said:

- But the sun is shining, uncle, and there are no clouds !!

That's not what I mean, son.

- I mean that -------

Behind them, in the introduction to the army and over the Iron Bull that was used over his dossier, I quickly looked back stopped the revolution, it was noted by (Cohen) and (CEO) that the data of the Tiger array is also, and they do not know why you stopped file as revolutionary, asked (CEO) reached curiosity has a large number of up to mountains:

- What is it, ma'am ?!

You didn't answer, but the long silence, until he thought that she wouldn't answer, never decided among himself that he hated hearing her question, but before it left his lips, the word she said suddenly:

- Tell the army to immediately.

After that, I said nothing. prompting (SEO) to cheer up by saying:

- Have we achieved our goal, Your Grace?

I haven't figured it out yet, but I was confused and told him firmly:

- Do it, captain. there is no need to speak.

And (Yazbek) adds one second, but let it go, the battle signal sounded quickly, get ready, and quickly went into the atmosphere, and yet, this huge city with high towers appeared, that the outlined body is huge, and was shown in the center by the door of a giant made of wood. colon, characterized by carvings of graceful and beautiful sculptures, he languished on the sides, depicting workers, so that in the immensity and beauty of those sitting on two seats, it was a masterpiece, characterized by the solidity and likelihood of the harsh, and within walking distance from it, pointed to the army of the queen standing, a proven dog in its place, silence fell on everyone.

In the sky, I took this screaming woman, with her harsh voice and whirling overhead, as if expecting something, I took the Raven, who landed on the stones scattered here and there, her sad cry, which goes through the psychology of grief and fear, and took some of the women coming and going by the faces of the soldiers who took impatiently and awaiting the orders of their queen. inside the one who took over the baton with her eyes, that the door to the huge double opens slowly, then a white flag comes out of one of the knights, and the escort trusts the iron through the horse until it stops in front of him, then got off him and bowed a little. growth, then thought and looked at the roll of leather that he carried in the folds of his clothes, and said:

- Tell this army .. and who owns lead and here, asking you, our king, the author of this great city to return to where you came from, and they escaped .. we do not want war in any form, and if you want it well .. welcome with your leader the guest strengthened by Macram, and if you want war .. you know that the city is not showing war for that, to understand if war is what you want, that you are chasing it, you know that the wind will be our ally, and Pisces has arrows of war, and death awaits in every grain of sand of your feet.

And then the knight finished his message, even forgotten, took it into his fist and waited for an answer, and a moment of silence passed between everyone, and suddenly she exhales revolutionary steam from her nose, and then lifts one of the front ones and quickly runs, and runs into the knight, who breathes his own immediately, did not expect this to happen !! And the Queen laughed brutally scary, as (Cohen) did, while proved (CEO) was in place and felt that his heart took the PM for the fate of this knight, and took the ghost of sadness invading his mind one little by little, said he himself, as he whispered, to prevent his queen; for he was afraid of his actions, like everyone else .:

"What should I have done, Your Grace.

She suddenly broke off her angry laugh and exclaimed in a harsh and terrible tone, as if I had heard:

- Shhhhh, bastard, do not forget that I am your master, I am the author of the people here, do not forget you, this is not for you, believe me.

Didn't reach (SEO) or speak, but was reluctant to say nothing while she added and she gave it back:

- I must go through this city; because the road is very long, because we don't want to get to it, and if we don't choose it, I won't get to it in time, but if you choose our path through this city, and of course you will save a lot of time.

He said (Seo) on a frequency clear in his tone:

- And .... And you .... But I'm not ma'am ..... I've never seen .....

The final (Cohen) quickly, smiling as if he had sold the king's decision, said the mischievously sly foxes:

- Yes, kind, your lordship, this is the best favor.

Then the silence continued as he looked at his friend with a meaningful sly look, he hates him and always wishes him company:

"Come on, my lady, there is no time to waste, go on our way to the council.

And then she laughed, trustingly raising her list, exposing the corpse of a knight and beginning to break bones completely, so that everything got confused, and led the army to continue on its way to this city with high towers without stopping, he saw the king of the city, what happened, and he fell heart between his legs, and his jaw fell down, he jumped in terror into the deepest depths inside him, the future became frightening for him and himself. ***

Suddenly (Strand) fell into the water violently, and dived to the bottom, and then rose to the surface, and felt that the current carried him away, and the place became dark, just like in the Jovi River, and fell (Lily), and the other quickly followed the file, which the last one stepped between them, and then accepted the challenge. :

- The (Lily) where are you?

I hear her calling us and saying:

- I'm here ..

And I heard two voices of your friend (Strand) say:

- And I too ..

I heard the voice of the king say:

- It looks like we are in the river, stupid, unreliable pulls us along.

Exclaimed (strand):

- It is very important that everything is good with us.

The king overheard adds:

- So far good.

Heard that Monday (Lily) that you're afraid of is popping up on her way to college:

"But the current seems to be accelerating as it progresses.

And on this the conversation ended, even taking the channel to steal more, and it took his movement to increase the pressure, and a faint light appeared in the distance, and the features of a place appeared in it, and there he tried three things that resisted the flash of water and held on to anything , and without further ado, for a group of protruding stones in the riverbed, groundwater, and took our companions to hunt in extreme violence, and for the Circle of Light, and for the clouds, and for the sky, and the king quickly exclaimed harshly, and he heard a roar water. :

- Looks like that waterfall .. grab whatever gets in your way.

And the fall of the king disappeared, and his voice with the sound of falling water, and followed her (Lily), that I could not hold on to anything, fell behind them (strand), in which case their fate was undeniably known or otherwise, but if I showed them a miracle ..

Yes, it's a miracle.

* * *

I downloaded the file of my organization once more to my eyes and looked at the army of the queen of darkness angrily said:

- As well as the war.

The concerned minister asked:

What happened, Milord ?!

Reduce the filesystem he said:

- I just killed the apostle ...

This was followed by a laparoscopic cast off his hand to fill the market bottom:

- Prepare the army .. it's time to fight.

Lift the weight of my hand and indicate where, and the soldiers quickly rose to the city wall with the arrows of their spears and waited for the moment of the attack, the king's minister told him: bend down:

Not a single gentleman is ready, sir, falls into bows, spears, the next delivery to the enemy, and the result is waiting impatiently ... do we have them now?

- No, wait for a signal from me.

Stop the file after the next scene based on the city wall, and at the same time your only desire, which is ...

(That movement never happens)

It was a desire to escape reality to the extreme.

* * *

A beetle in the air changed oil .. announcing the beginning of a battle between the army of darkness and the army of this city, and that the supposed Army of darkness was from them and became in the crosshairs, so the king ordered to shoot arrows and spears towards the king and his army, and soon began to improve in the sky, and peered at his target, like an army of black flies, although they raised their shields to prevent them, but this did not stop the arrows from reaching them, he took some blows so quickly and for a long time in the necks and legs, eyes, arms, and some of them were killed, another took another rose in the ground, distracted from the severity of pain, and why stop there ?! But they screamed in anger and then continued on their way to the city wall ..

They lift wooden ladders, you climb them taking the city's army, throwing arrows, spears and pushing the ladder away from the marketplace, Wilton's fire on the heads of the Dark Army and the scene was horrible as hell and described the revolution iron to the massive wooden door and took it cruelly with her, and after a few minutes he took the door crack here is a file with a note to hand over to the army of darkness inevitably, he shouted at his minister, he stands on one of the towers that allow him to see everything below that is in the power of anger has a pole of its brow:

- Ask the military specialist ... this time ... she's quick.

The priest shouted to one of them:

- And they shot the army, etc.

He shouted out another similar phrase, and the last one, and suddenly the gates swung open a giant wooden city appeared what was behind it, this is an army of giants and green-skinned greens !!, they looked more like people in an external configuration, armed with sharp swords and large shiny shields, then they set off with confident steps to stand in front of the gate, and the moments passed, it took the soldiers of darkness, who looked at the giants in indecision and fear, suddenly shouted (catfish style) with shouts of the strong frequency of the soldiers' blow and made their attack furious and vicious, but the giant was in that that they were destroying them everywhere like flocks of flies !! , With one blow she shaved many of them in the sky and fell away, broke their heads and legs, and their hands mixed with warm blood, and in a fierce battle she took it to the maximum, and moments passed ... even jumping out of the pile of corpses under her feet giants, the starting tiger array in a respite of knowledge and in the fight became a frightening and frightening extreme.

* * *

Having cleared the cave of stone color, sadly and furiously pushing the water, this was the last scene that our Three heroes see and they fall from the waterfall, which reached a height of a thousand meters, was mixed with water, and when they thought that death was inevitably approaching with its end , the last thing you can imagine happened, whichever view went to their horses !! Before the end of several meters, he put three into the air from the hollow of the waterfall, the sound of his radar is the last deafening, like that of Juarez, thousands and thousands of bulls are raging, and suddenly all of them felt that something could catch on to them tightly, and then take them away from this great waterfall.

They rise into the sky and their hearts are beating hard, not believing that they have survived certain death ?!, glanced at the scene of the waterfall, this is a note I (Lily) - a wonderful sight !! And there are many giant birds that enter the waterfall and love to hunt their food from them !! And then she flew away somewhere far, far away, and horror boiled when she saw that the one who carried it was a bird from this exotic bird, this bird became extinct in the era of the dinosaurs ... this is a plane with reptiles, and he looked around around and saw that another bird was holding salt and (staff) that he wondered in fear he looked at the ground below in horror filled his entire being:

- Where are we being taken, these winged creatures? We're getting out of ... where are we going?

I took these flying reptiles flying in the sky above the clouds, when over the mountains, while others, and over the valleys of deserts, forests, rivers, and in such a case, even passed over the city with high towers and statues from a huge stone were carved brilliantly like no other, as it seems like there is a war going on to revolve at the bottom, and if the crawler carrying (Lilia) maybe it will be a war.) A little battlefield ... to warm up her brother and uncle between the bars of the Great Cage, and within a few minutes the city is visible and appeared after a small lake in the valley of the doomed among the mountains, and discovered a lake that emerged after the great desert, and after a period of choosing a desert began to show green trees gradually, after a period of exploration. The back lake is Big and very big ..

So many, that the king did not believe that the same was visible !! He had this largest lake that he had seen in his life, stretched along and across every object and species of beautiful wild animals, from deer there were, as well as trees and flowers of different sizes and colors, and birds with sounds, sparkling colors, and the bird flew over a lake with clear water, so that it discovered these sunken temples at the bottom, this huge multicolored fish, this giant turtle that swims in silence, approached these reptiles from the surface of the lake to such an extent that our companions felt the splashing of water on their faces.

In the distance, a large city appeared in the center, with domes of a high color of gold, the story with tall towers of various shapes here and there, and taking the sun slowly changed, acquiring a search page of this orange color, and enjoyed the golden domes more, and this reptile of the city, so I climbed up at a sharp angle, suddenly made (Lilly) more, and flew until I reached the largest building in the city, then I landed in a wide area, and threw them into a rage, and then stood next to them, making a noise. for Max, for example, to announce her arrival.

The king tried to get up and looked around ... and found that this place was square, flowers blooming here and there, and streams of magnificent fountains, and marble statues, white, pink and invariably great, said to his companions:

- Looks like guys are approaching this station ..

- She (Lily) exclaimed, so as not to stop her friend, and looked around:

- We survived death ... and only God knows our fate in this place.

Suddenly a huge door opened, dug with marvelous inscriptions, was strewn with diamonds and precious stones, and behind him a white man with a mustache, a short beard, and lined up strangely gradually, replacing gold and precious stones, and hoisted a golden crown over his head, a gray-haired man, was dressed in dark - a red suit, decorated with golden threads, which meant prosperity, and behind it stood a group of people in the form of horsemen, and quietly approached them, and stood in front of them, accepting the need carefully and silently.

A long silence worried him and frightened and terrified him, and after a few minutes it seemed to me that an eternity had passed with ours, what was this man worth ... and what he said was a surprise for everyone !! ...

* * *

They attacked the army of giants, they brutally kill everyone who fights with them mercilessly or mercifully, and they roar with powerful sounds and screams, and during this terrible fight ... one of them fell at the feet of the Iron Bull, who put his hoof over the head of a giant, broken terribly, clogged with blood !!, and trustingly hovers from his nose, as if bragging about what he did, and then attacked the giant, the last and the last, and he knocks them down. to the right and to the left, and with their feet simply, they crush bones, shout loudly and loudly, and attack the army of the city in full force against the army of darkness, and shoot spears and arrows everywhere, reaching the sky, until they almost block the light of the sun, like armies of big blacks flies.

All this did not stop the army from advancing, even for a moment !! And he took a body that was flowing profusely, and the blood was hot throughout the place, and the city quickly became terrible under the feet of the Iron Ox, as well as colossal statues and towers, and caught fire in all places, even women and children did not have mercy on them with trust or tiger eyes, and remained so. read the first, and in the end another tower will fall, and there will be nothing there but ruins, above the plateau of rubble. I climbed on a bull, and over the body of a small child, clutching the palm of a mother who passed away from a completely different life, stop and let out a whining roar and renew his steam, as if he knows that the NFL is his with a stone heart, and the end of the city authorities need .. Steel piles of ash and rubble, the ruins are destroyed, there were no tall towers and palaces, gardens and full of men, women and children one day, and taking the bull exhausted and asks his head to the right and left, and taking the disk of the Sun changes into the slow, heralded end of the city with the end of the day.

* * *

Widened eyes (burgundy) and almost tears fall from them, and he looks at everything around him, and exclaims that he took grief from them the amount that he thinks his little heart is strong:

- You mean it, uncle? ... Do you mean this autumn?

Book of the Damned (Episode 9) armies are terrible
The army of darkness liquidated the city assembly and crushed it in full.

The creature shook his head and answered melancholy and contrite:

- Yes, sonny, this is what I say, it is the damned king who comes with her, wherever you are, and clings to grapple with her and knock the devil out of her head so that she becomes his companion, but the leader according to his own whims and ideas that came from hell.

Grasp (burgundy) the bars of the cage tighter, and he had a tear on the hot end ... like lava from an erupting volcano, and exclaimed, looking at the remains of this city:

"They wiped out the city from the face of the earth, her father, and, having taken pity and pity even on children and the elderly, they will not leave anyone, crushing every stone.

The silence of this thing took its owner for the next scene; the vapors rose from these ruins, the smell of death spread everywhere, here the voice of the annoying one had to take the floor, as if he knew his anger, he had a thing on his head, trying to calm him down and said::

- May be .

Commented on (tanning) this dog was shot even before she sobbed, and then everyone fell silent ... and take the Southern darkness waiting among the ruins of the city they are plundering ... indifferent to the corpses that fell everywhere in an awful variety.

* * *

Stop this king in front of our heroes, and look at them carefully, then stand on your rack with the ghost of a small smile, which he said:

- Welcome to my second ..

I sighed (Lily) sobs Lane, she felt that a heavy mountain could come off her chest, gesture him (wise) with the same smile and then he said, holding out his hand to:

"I was honored to see you, sir.

"That's right, trust me ... judging by your appearance, you are from the height of your people, right?

Answer (wise):

"It looks like Your Majesty understands the system.

The extended smile file said that it refers to the act where the seats are very beautiful, there is a carved carpet of great beauty, with tall glass windows that a ray of sun entered, pollution in colors and graphics accepts the contract:

- If there is a story behind you, I would like to hear it .. sit down, have a drink and listen to their story.

And everyone gathered in a council and took their places, and began to reign (wise) stories about that merchant and (Lily), then they supplemented her story and called her intently, and opened their mouths for a while ... and raised their eyebrows while the other, as uncertified, she even finished her story, and everyone fell silent, as if expecting more, and the king exclaimed:

- What is this wonderful tale ?!

The modern did not follow, but he continued, rising from his council:

- You are over the head with guests, and rest during the day, and tomorrow we'll talk in order (book of the damned)

Then he ordered three rooms and new clothes to be equipped for them, after which he left them and left for the affairs of his kingdom.

* * *

Sat (AJ) around the fire, which was kindled, and individual cards and captures were seen in attention to the authority of the people dancing in front of him, the light was reflected on his face, as if ghosts were jumping back and forth ... and then he said to himself:

- It looks like we did a lot of what we wanted, but not so much until we get everything we want and ....

Then the silence continued and his eyes widened dramatically.

- Take the book ... and then ...

Silence again, and then a crazy man exclaimed loudly:

- And then the whole world will be mine.

Taking sound in endless space non-stop, carrying with them insane hopes, someone else wants to dictate the world ..

Yes, he wants to have it, not one other may have it one day, and all his predecessors, who thought that they paid dearly for crazy, but very dearly more than you imagine, it was always the price of their life, and they became a footnote in the forehead of time

A memory, and nothing else.

* * *

(Lily) stood on this terrace with wonderful sculptures and friezes, a beautiful golden look at this sight is possible without end, then little by little changes follow the sun into this world to save the New World, and there are birds flying back to their nests in their daily travel, and then dismissed, holding them too far away ... remembering my brother without thinking about his fate, and such a situation (wise) Wang waza's hand laid on her shoulder, but when she turned to notice this horror, replaced his smile, which melted her heart, he said to her, looking into her eyes:

"I'm sorry I scared you and broke into your loneliness ... knowing that I knocked too much on the door; but you seem to be not here.

- No, you don't need to apologize.

- You thought you didn't feel my penetration here ?!

- Yes, I thought about my brother and his fate.

- I wished her well ... God forbid to meet again.

A sigh, and in the distance, already there, tears met her:

I would like to.

Try (wisely) to make it a little easier for him and tell him something; but suddenly he entered (the staff), shouting irritably, and let you recognize his face:

- You are here and do not know what is happening around you ?!

Exclaimed (sage) has the pole of his forehead:

- What's the matter?

- In the big clock that stands in front of the Palace, preparations are underway for the big test, there is an unusual movement everywhere, let's look at it.

The three of them set off until they reached Velikaya Square, past the huge sculptures of the customer, flowering plants that spread beautiful works of art here and there, and there they saw the king to cheer up their warriors, who put on an enlarged combat uniform of their fantastic and their blue color, and helmets exquisite work already stood in orderly rows. :

- Oh, southern oh, shaking the ground under your feet ... the roar of Pisces on their voices, do not underestimate your enemy and the world speaks about you easily, and grabbed your intestines, and your women, your children say, and guard your land and for yours proposal, they fought to the death, and that right with you ... and wait for your enemy on the form of the city, their spears and forge your swords, he takes you by mercy or respite or pity, and they know that your children are used to waiting for us with victory, which trembles over your head and rubs your hands. the path with roses, history awaits you the author of the example to the Great in the letters of Nur on his timeless forehead, do not fail them and return them to her, take your hearts and in the whole deep well, there is a weakness with that ... come back for her.

And his successor led his army to shout in a voice that thundered and shook the mountains:

- About victory .... Victory .... Victory

- Three of our friends are silently watching what is happening, unaware of what is happening, - said the King (sage):

- What's going on here today?

- The soldier answered quickly. :

- This is war, sir !!

- I exclaimed, saying:

- The war between whom and whom?

- The war between crazy US money and crazy Earth.

- Why is this war between you and you from a sexual one?

Book of the Damned (Episode 9) armies are terrible
Clothes on the side, from the finest and most luxurious war clothes in the story.
- Sir, the war has been going on for many years, the length of our lives, so everyone is sure that it will never end for one, the reason is in these trees that grew on the shore of the lake, it is very rare that they exist only almost here, and bear fruit only once in a hundred years, this fruit from eating is cured of any disease, God forbid !! And many years ago, abundant health and youth, and the fact that these trees grew on our lake ... they have the right to cherish its use, but the departed Earths see that this is their right, this is not the right to have its fruits they grew on the earth, they are within its borders, and therefore it remained a war between two teams without victory for either of them.

Let go of the file (wisely) with his mind a little he said:

- What a war !!

- Any other services, sir?

A smile (wise) told him :,

"Thank you, soldier.

Almost the soldier is gone; but the owner of the club returned again, stood in front of him and said:

- Yes, sir .

Hem, and then he said:

- May I ask you? for what?

- Yes, sir .

- So your ear doesn't even hear us one of them.

Kill his soldier and whisper Do not serve ... and shook the soldier's head to approve, and set off smiling to tell me a few minutes after holding his hands and clothes similar to the uniforms of soldiers, put them in the hands of the king, who went to (Lily) and (the staff) said to them:

- Were wearing this outfit.

- Exclaimed the first, quickly:

- You want us to fight with them ?!

He replied, its owner:

- Why not?

- I shouted in his face. :

- Are you out of your mind ?! .. Do you want to succeed by dying in the form of a city of spears as part of postponing this war ?!

- How do you say that? All I wanted was to give something in return to those who helped us pay for it.

Left (Lily) is cool about it and she says:

"But that's not how we react to everyone, there are many ways others see them.

Boycotted (by the wise), he approached them and with a beautiful voice acts in their hearts:

- I agree with you .. but if you repeat that we are thus the biggest and most beautiful casts us.

There was silence and there was silence .. and I took Buddy, our thoughts, and then she turned to look at him extended the system, and suddenly a piece (thread) of rope silence, saying::

- Oh, are we going to wear this outfit or not?

The king (sage) looks at (Lily) as if he was waiting for an answer from them, and after a few seconds he thought that a refusal would be her answer, so he decided to say something, but she said that she was running back to him and to the army of sex:

- I hate war in general and I want to divide it, and did not imagine that one day I would be there in an intensified battle of my new life and live until tomorrow's sun.

After a pause, he continued:

- I.....

Silence again, and then turned around and painted a beautiful smile on her face, and she quickly says:

- I'll be there for you .

Smile file (wise) said, his heart beats happily:

- I almost lost hope in you.

Look at them (the staff) and he feels that there is something invisible that unites these two .. something that matters to everyone and not big with eyes, but he understands that he smiled correctly and said:

- Let's not waste time if she is wearing an outfit to take with her.

The starting Troika in the hallways of the palace has not yet disappeared from sight, and the thunderous screams of soldiers have not frozen in the air

- Victory ..

Taking pictures hesitate to stop him.

* * *

Why does the sun shine after it spreads a haze in the air, calmed, the search page completely and the silence of it all, seeped this fog between huge trees, made it look like the ghosts of giants, the silent sentries of this place, and the heart of a photograph showing an army of goblins is water as if it appears from nowhere, and they are holding spears, and swords, and nobility, and their king in front of one of the battalions, and the soldiers escaped from our heroes, the light of the Sun leaks to shame ... and the Sword of King Jin in the water reflected the light of the sun ... and during the lull he raised his head to the sky to see how these giant birds accompanied his army, and one of his soldiers sits above him, holding a fork by the middle of his team, dismounts, walks through the horse a few steps to become in the forefront of his army and then shouted to them a strong voice roared, brandishing his sword for them:

- Fight like a man and do not hold back ... defend your honor at all costs, and know that victory awaits you after defeating your enemy, and that shame and shame await you, if you fall, do not let him take his chance.

And at this cry, all the soldiers excitedly waved their hands up and vigorously shook him:

- Victory ... victory ... victory

And then silence everything and fog little by little, I took the pictures to unfold slowly, and the army of the goblins of the earth stood looking at them far away, he stood in front of them, their king rode, and rose like an army to his shield and helmet with inscriptions that all the bends are in green , sparkling, behind the army stood giant dinosaur-like creatures with a long neck, being huge, and above her head, a small hat, one of the soldiers to control them, and now and then took these creatures with a growling voice intimidating, and what if she saw (Lily) this scene is legendary, she even exclaimed, was glad to have eyebrows in her body and mind:

- Lord of everything .. Where did these great creatures come from?

The Goblin King cut off the money for his silence and exclaimed forcefully In the South:

"Don't let the sight of them scare you and shake your heart, your heart are the hearts of brave knights who don't want to die and throw bales, and they are the strongest here.

Silence followed the attack on Hamas by its soldiers and then added even more:

- The holder of the right is always the strongest, do not shake his size - this is his enemy ... the drum roll even sells their hearts strongly, and they are afraid of the decay of their bodies and weakens their minds.

The frequency of the sound of the drums resonates strongly in the air, here again the king exclaimed, and he is still swinging his sword in the air:

- Don't suggest any steps. but they ignored the arrows inside the brackets inserted into spears and swords and waited for the signal to attack.

Taking the sound of drums resonating in the atmosphere and all the products at the site of their king's signal, and minutes passed, passed like years, and without further ado, over the beats at the end of his green feather, to settle in the heart of one of the soldiers, to die in the course, and the King's eyes did not pass a second, they even missed, the sky overhead was filled with arrows of the goblin earth, raising the goblin water shields over their heads to protect them, and after the wave of arrows died down, the king ordered after a while even ... and hit the road. the arrows of the goblin flew like a fly into the light of the sun from the enemy, and, having landed them, the king shouted after her:

- Come on guys, get under way

Leading the warriors with vigorous cries from strong shaking hearts, and after that the arrows ended, the sky appeared, even an army of goblins was sent into battle from the other side, neighbors joined the screams of battle, and blood was taken to appear everywhere, and swords rang, and into the air giant birds and stones were taken to fly at enemies, while I took this huge living creature that swooped down on everything that came in its path, and bodies were taken falling apart and dripping without stopping, but I took an increase

AND

He stopped

It was the easiest thing for them, it seemed that the battle would never end.

* * *

I am the Sun in the sky, and the temperature of the air, with grains of sand under the feet of the army of darkness, he makes his way in this desert, perhaps, but the end is difficult, the cut of the thirst of their lips, they fall one after the other from excess, exhaustion, thirst, lose their meager water, and the fall leaves him to the predators, and they took to continue walking, and they stagger, and suddenly a voice screams, he refers to these birds that fly over the valley between the ridge of small mountains:

- M

Watch the beauty and Dubai in action, when you see birds flying there, they know this bird should fly over the Oasis as you can there, a dog walking with energy and almost a smile on their faces and touched their hearts that something comforting; because they thought they would die of thirst between the folds of the desert, the only file that did not utter a word, but remained silent, clearing these mountains with their sharp eyes, as if there is something the same that no one knows about others.

See what this thing is in itself ?!
In the respite of the war between the sexes ... take the file (wise), Boyko fights and miraculously on the battlefield, already accepting the knock of the sergeant's hand with his sword, and now the sword penetrates the body without stopping and mercy, I took the warm blood that appears here, then there and all around him, and his face, and there is one second to catch his breath, as if he had become a machine, accustomed inexorably, and during his desperate fight ... found one south of the goblin land and stood in front of him, refusing from sex, his face turned a bright color, he saw the owner and quickly raised his sword to say that he hit him hard in the heart and eyes, before piercing the king with his sword, he suddenly stopped .. As if he saw the puck and gave up his place , and bowed his sword, and blood dripped from his blade, and everyone around him was so busy defending, and a few seconds passed, and took a firing squad on Monday, some silently and forgot that they were in the theater of operations.

- Exclaimed the file (Wise) in amazement and lost weight to a painted face:

- It's you?!
The Queen stood with an army in front of this calm lake and silently looked at her, as if she wanted to penetrate its dark depths with a sharp knife, but her warriors were thirsty .. so they did not care about the position of their queen from the base, but quickly rode to the beach and took a drink water with a heavy binge hyper his thirst, while taking one tiger with a sound annoying and offers (CEO) tries to calm him down, the Tiger of the other also takes the same position, taking a roaring voice annoying and tries to get away from this place, or (Burgundy) if we came closer and entered

the ranks of the soldiers .. In our opinion, the Sheikh (Abdullah) holds a cane next to him, and there the dog barks aggressively both at the bars of the cage and at his head, he is wearing a thing on his head and says to the owner::

- Our friend seems to see that something is bothering him !!

Look (burgundy) through the bars. he said he was surprised:

- There seems to be something unusual; and the net too, And here they are in front of the lake - fresh water quenches their thirst.

Raise this thing to his head in the air and say:

"Maybe animals see money the same way we see you, son.

"I know, sir, but maybe nothing important, uncle.

Following the sheikh he said:

"Or maybe it's something important for my son.

Then silence finally came, and taking the dog barking nonstop, and moving away from them ... and on the lake shore, in particular, the soldiers took a drink and washed their faces with cold water, and they smiled, taking several bottles filled with it to quench their thirst after that, during a busy Friday, something happened to the movement of the water violently !! And you can notice that one of the soldiers approached his colleague and said to her in a deep voice:

- Did you see that?!

He replied to his colleague with a smile:

- What did you see?!

He pointed first to the surface of the lake and said to him:

- Look, can't you see this fog ?!

Look at the lake a second time and said in a funny way:

- I wonder if there is fog in the middle of the day?! .. Is it really true?

And he ended his last conversation, even taking on the surface of the water a highly vibrating, strong and light haze from bubbles. as if the lake was boiling, and all the soldiers of the command and their eyes, they say (Sioux), are trying to control the tiger:

- Ma'am, what exactly is going on here?

I looked at him said the King to calm the nerves of the wondrous:

"I order everyone to retreat immediately and move away from the lake.

In vain (CEO) at that time and did not even think about it, his soldiers cried, saying:

- Move back, immediately leave the lake.

Book of the Damned Episode 10 (Return of the Missing)
It was the spell of Jafar the giant sea octopus !!
Fear and blasphemy arose among the soldiers, which caused what was happening to the lake, they rushed at a fast run away from the lake shore, during which the queen ordered to retreat, and the tiger walked away and made a noise, but suddenly one of the

soldiers remembered that he had left his bottle on the shore, he said to his friend and he quickly took a breath. :

- I forgot my bottle on the beach.

The assistant quickly shouted, he raises his eyebrows:

- Don't even think about coming back !!

He said quickly and turned his back to the shore:

- And what can you say besides this?

Dude you have a teammate, but he didn't hear it, he needed to run down until he reached the place where you left your bottle, pick it up very quickly to return to the page with your army again, drawing the eyes of what something quickly moving along the surface of the lake, or to its place and took the next scene, and in turn this thing even faster, he ate the horror of his heart and shot his feet in the wind, taking the focus of the dropped bottle from his hand and not taking care of it, and shouted just right to the guy who stopped to give him, and he widened his eyes in horror, while a smile appeared on his face first, which quickly disappeared when he looked into the eyes of my teammate, who opened his mouth and in horror was already standing in its place is different and, wrapping something around the center, signed everything !! Taking dog tracks in the silence of this scene, frightening and terrifying as much as one can imagine, here exclaimed (Burgundy), who had already taken horror into his blood, like water that flows in a lake:

- Chapter "Wow!" what it is?!!!

The answer sounded in a terrifying sense of the word.

* * *

His eyes widened with a file (wise), which, apparently, interfered in front of him, and the hard eternity of minutes passed, and then a smile and he says:

- Is it reasonable ?! ... A set of dice?

He replied that he held out his hand to help him up:

- Sir, is it reasonable that I see you here ?!

D the king helped him up with his hand, then hugged him tightly and, looking into his face, he had already forgotten about the war:

"I missed you so much that we thought we had lost you beyond the bounds.

Smile (catfish style) said:

- Age of apartments is the rest, sir.

He looked at the king and asked if his smile had disappeared:

- But how did you survive death ?!

"It's a long story, sir.

Silence, and then the king asked:

- But what brings you here, my lord, with the big money ?! Where is (strand) and (Lily) ??

The king smiled and said:

- Why is this a long story and now is not the time for stories?

Exclaiming (catfish style), he looked around.

- What should we do now? And yet after the fight ?!

- The King answered firmly and quickly made a decision. :

"No more fighting today ... let's stop this war at all costs.

Another exclaimed, raising his eyebrows:

- Like this?!

The king exclaimed loudly:

"We're trying to stop everyone from fighting.

Look at these two together, as if each of them reads what is in the blood of the other, and then loudly shouts to them in turn and in a strong voice:

- Stop

Photographing leaves many in endless space and between soldiers, but to stop.

* * *

The Sheikh (Abdullah) who exclaimed, reached his ears with his frightening cry, Yes, so much that they fluttered his conscience and forced him to wear Said:

- What's the matter, son?! ... What happened, son? What is the secret of this terrible conflict ?!

Answered (tan) his eyes widened in horror and he took in the amount of fear:

- He is such a big monster of freedom that I have seen in my life ?!

He grabbed the creature by the shoulder (tan) said:

- Jesus Christ .. save me from this terrible situation do not leave us.

- It's a pity that you can't see his uncle .. this is the biggest giant octopus you might not even see in your nightmares, it is distinguished by long arms and sticky places, where there are many terrible pipettes, and two eyes get horror from everywhere.

He kidnapped this soldier's octopus from his belt, wrapped it with one hand and then swung to the water, the dog watched this scene in horror, the soldier screamed, and I took the rest of his hands and hit it and got stuck, and there was a terrible state of hupla, and I grabbed one hands of the tiger, who all the time tried to get rid of them with all his might, and put his rider on the ground, and Tiger II jumped away from the hands of the base, the Queen stood still, watching the scene in silence, and suddenly without any prefaces. cry file cry great in the south and she says:

- Attack the soldiers, do not retreat, they have thrown fear away from you and have the courage of heroes.

And so the king threw these words of protection between its southern sides, so that I walked among them, as if by magic, charges were spears, swords and catapults on this huge monster, which he flew into a rage, taking him eight everywhere he could reach , etc. from the tiger that held him and ran away and accepted the scary sounding call, after a period of attack and pressure .. Having taken the position of the monster's retreat, he retreats into the background and the links and the soldiers will attack you even more, increasing their response enthusiasm, and will return to the water until he does something extraordinary for a huge monster, like in front of these little soldiers for him, he dived into the water and disappeared completely, and the soldiers looked at the water, not believing in what happened before them, minutes later, the soldiers thought, they won this battle, and that victory was their ally, then they shouted victory cries, they took the jumps as a small joy, their victory, and did not know what it was. What awaited them in the future after that.

* * *

In the very heart of the lake in this Sheikh specially ... his goblin king money on a round table with fantastic carvings, in front of him sat the goblin king earth, his beard is large white and his body is full, and sat to the right of the king (sage), and behind him stood (Lily) and (Stranga) and (sum model), during a meeting with some of the princes and leaders, took the floor to speak and they nervously and listening to some of them, there a file (wise) rose from his place and hit the table surface with his fist and shouted:

- Enough ...

Everyone fell silent and looked at him, continuing to say:

"We came here to end this war and to listen to some, there is no need to waste time on words, not one of them is meaningless.

He was interrupted by the Goblin King Money, saying in anger:

The trees to our right are crazy money ... for no one else.

Hop the Goblin King of the Earth from his seat, speaking in anger:

- How can you say that?! If the fruits of our right.

Garden Pandemonium again, take the wrath of the end of their hearts, and they take turns ... and banged on the table, that's said (Lily), directed her conversation to (staff):

- It seems that the owner will cope with his mission ..

- Need exclaimed angrily:

- Never fails.

She told him it was raising one of her eyebrows and the ghost of a crooked smile on her lips:

"We'll watch for a bit.

Then I passed the baton to the Queen (sage), who shouted back in anger:

- Stop

They all fell silent again, and the Beetle looked at him in silence with his face angrily, he said to them:

"You don't need to talk to Wong about some, let's listen to some of the pure ones, your scourge children of this war that have no place.

Doesn't follow someone something, but they discovered a health product to say the file you end with a saying:

- It seems that these trees are located in the neutral zone ....

He got the dog, hearing his conversation, took the floor to speak and protest, here is (Lily's) smile for (a strand of) fun with which he became angry and his eyes and tried to say something, but his control over his character and the subsequent scene again says:

- Listen to me ..

"Again the silence of the dog," he continued. :

- Yes, first listen to me ... and if I didn't say words like you, then speak, discuss and come to a decision.

Book of the Damned Episode 10 (Return of the Missing)
The file wise work of the truce between the side (elf) and the war is over forever.
Orgasm them with their heads with approval, start giving your words, saying:

Since the trees are in a neutral place ... better think about how we use these trees for my benefit to you two? Let's take a truce for five years, even produced through which the trees will bear fruit in half between the two of you, and create this agreement that will vary by right and nothing, and above all the idea that they were in two parts, and the number of families, who lost their shepherd, and how a mother became an orphan for her children, how my son expects that his father will return from this war no more, the war will not only lead and retreat to the rear, will invite the people to live in peace, invite them to think about how build it? ... How to end and progress towards world peace? Not a war ..

Silence of the king, and the Goblin King took the money to talk to the followers just like the Goblin did the land, and then stopped suddenly gave the file (wise), said to them::

- Ha ... What do you think?

The Goblin King's gaze turned to his opponent, one eyebrow raised and his mustache twisted, and everyone thought he would refuse, but he exclaimed:

- Good !!

Stop with a smile said the Goblin King of Earth:

- I `m alright too !!

Shake hands with two smiling people, look (strand) at (Lily) in healing, what her face is, thereby bringing peace to our companions between Jin water Jin land, and end this war, which lasted for years without stopping.

* * *

Above this rock, a stop (AJ) with his horse can be seen endlessly on the landscape, and the expanded vision saw one of the mountains as high as:

- I suggested to our dear and do not part me with you a lot, feeling your cards in the palm of your hand, and my eyes will be your words.

Then type that the patient looks ahead, as he would look at his system, and should paint on his face the ghost of the smile of a cunning demon who came from hell.

* * *

Suddenly and without preamble ... come out of this giant octopus of water, and attack the army of the Queen of Darkness again and take them down everywhere, and their rocks without mercy, so that, in the struggle of throats, and to stop the Queen of

Darkness from looking at him without speaking, while I took the octopus in my Hands, beat it with all my might and everything that came its way, and then ordered the revolutionary iron to attack it, and you are Monday, and flew to the Tsarina in the air, high and far from the revolutionary, and gave the octopus confidence .. and threw him by hand into the cage that housed his father's tombs. master, shouted when he saw the bull rushing towards the world:

- And his !!

Lost his fight and cage tightly, and gained confidence and rushed to fight again, steam came out of his nostrils, like an angry volcano, leaving behind his own (burgundy). The one who rose from the fragments of its leaves asked for a thread of blood from his head and mouth, and perhaps felt that the world around him was restless, and a headache, a terrible throbbing in his head, but he quickly regained his balance and he was able to control his limbs, and looked around looking for his uncle, heard the barking of dogs, gave his hand, found him standing next to his uncle, who wore it on his stomach, a punch in his direction, and fear that it could take the collapse of his heart, let him bend I don't see how he can do it. is .:

- Uncle, are you okay ?!

She obeyed him and tried to examine him .. he said Do not breathe intermittently cut hearts:

- No time, boy, it's time to finally leave.

Look at those tears in his eyes, and he looks at his chest, he surrendered to the great greatness of the cell, which parted from him to settle in his chest, has significantly spread to the blood ..

- Don't cry, son, go and leave me here.

- No, I won't leave you here.

- Don't do this ... this is good tea, skinned after the massacre, Run, son, Don't miss this opportunity.

He removed the hand of the creature (burgundy) and, remembering his last breath, shouted:

- Run away ... run away ..

Stop (Burgundy) and be in supreme sorrow over the fate of this thing, then the linear two-stage looked at him again and found he was dead !! Returned to him quickly and hugged him and took his crying and crying, and the heavy seconds passed for eternity .. Then she suddenly stopped and laid him on the ground and slowly fell, taking the dog wagging her tail next to her and her voice like a face, then started on Monday after leave the army, ready to substitute them to fight this huge and terrible sea monster, and suddenly lit the queen's scepter with a superimposed light sight, and stopped everything After, then returned the light to twilight disappeared along with this sea monster, then returned the file to the back of the bull with iron, and I pass a lake that takes water to boil and disappear over time until it disappears completely. Completely disappearing, taking the rest of the army trying to get up and re-create the page, they left their wounded as usual and continued on their way as if nothing had happened to them.

* * *

Sel (the sage) and his companions on this terrace with marble sculptures, magnificent climbing plants and flowers of different colors, Accept stands against the background of this beautiful lake, sunlight is reflected on her mythical page, they listen (catfish model) and she says:

- When he fell off the cliff and lifted the watch's face (Lily) smiling to the top and I just sank to the bottom, so I thought the end was near, but I fell into the water and I found myself drifting with the flow, and I thought I had survived a fall into the water, despite my desperate attempts to get out .. the current was very high and I took a hit on the rocks until I started to faint, and took the appearance that it was all camouflaged and I saw a group of huge animals who were collecting money to run, and then one of them opened his mouth and jumped out with huge teeth and met me on the spot, and darkened the lower part of consciousness completely.

* * *

The term of this huge animal the owner of a long neck (catfish model) suddenly came out of his mouth, the owner of his eye to avoid the sunlight of the force; his eyes cannot bear the light of the sun; he stayed in the mouth of this creature for a long time, then raised his hand over his eyes until it softened a little light, even regained the ability to see and explain the scene more, it was all about his supplier, and found a group of people around him staring at him in amazement , and overheard someone say it refers:

This is a man.

Try to look at them clearly, even a trace of their features, but he encountered difficulties in a clearer vision, he watched them as if they were people of his features, I took the vision includes gradually revealing their features, they were three people them with big eyes of the same color of green, drooping ears on both sides, and oval whites try the presence of angels, and people are long white draped behind their backs, their clothes, laced with bright colors, said the owner wondering what they were:

- Where I am?

- You are in our land, you are a man.

Try (adder) stand up and ask again:

- What country is this ?!

Answered the latter said:

- You're in your village ...

He was interrupted by the first of them, saying:

- Better go to King Linda in it.

The silence of the three was a bit like how they think, and then the middle one said:

- You're right ... you better go on business.

Book of the Damned Episode 10 (Return of the Missing)
The side of the Earth, the best and most beautiful land I have ever seen ... has a good abundance, and women also enjoy all the wonderful ..
Help three (catfish style) to stand on the stand, then order one of these huge animals with a specific workmanship on the ground, and stepping on the back of his master, accompanied by another, focused the other two animals and left, heading to his king's palace. and did not know its owner until now who they were, and not for what purpose, but after many hours of walking under the rays of the Holocaust sun ... they reached a huge forest of tall trees and with intertwined branches, and, having penetrated into it, he saw its owner is a bunch of ghosts, jumping here and there. there, among the branches, and he thought it was a flock of monkeys, or maybe a group of ferrets, and clicked on it .. He saw that the sun's

rays could not penetrate the branches, tangled and lush, spread out in multi-colored bird trills among the branches, and every now and then believed that the animals sound scary, however, with the puffing features of these ghosts that pranced among the branches, they are a bunch of children of different ages, similar in shape That is, with their crisp whiteness, and their eyes are green and clear, and they looked at him in surprise, and some of them threw their fruits, and every now and then they caused high laughter, and from under the trunks of these trees a large city appeared. , carved houses and mansions with glass windows and an exquisite house, stood all the way to the owners Knee goes to the royal palace, which was occupied by the largest tree trunks, the longest, close it, stop the animal that protects its owner, and then backwater and plant its owner and even standing in front of a man by his features, we know that he is old, puts a crown of gold and diamonds on his head, the education of a vegan, the whole product adorns his face and a few gold coins could be put in a white beard, and from his hand he takes a green twig with leaves of a flower quite ripe, he was next to his woman until she becomes his wife. almighty God in beauty !! Even with her gray hair tucked behind her back, next to his flamingo is another .. A young man stood in the prime of an athlete and exquisite colors and patterns, bowed to two men before their king, and stopped (catfish style) saw that he was impressed by this place, and as it happens, remaining king, he turned his conversation to the owner of our house. :

- Welcome, my son, to our house ..

Then he smiled and held out his hand to score a goal:

"You do us the honor.

The frequency of its owner, therefore, hoped to force him to come here in order to meet a warm welcome, but he did not think so, but he already trusted to shake hands with the king:

"Actually, it's an honor for me, Milord.

The king brought him to the palace and said to him:

- We asked for an excuse for our children if they were arranged by you in an inappropriate way.

I did not hear his master, he looked around and was surprised at what he sees inside this palace !! It was the most beautiful thing that can be seen in a person in his life, he was adorned with dresses, curtains, statues, covered with diamonds and gold in all places, and took to say no:

- I would like to welcome you to our country, son ... a country, a bygone land.

And the withered owner seemed to have been struck by lightning and exclaimed:

- The land of the goblins ?!

- Yes, son of the Land of Goblins ... and I feel your fear of this unnecessary, we are peaceful and do not like to offend others, and the welcome guest is cream shorter, no matter how long your stay there lasts.

- I want to introduce you to my son (Sands) ... he is the only one I have.

Not to mention his master, as if a cat had eaten his tongue, he chased after the king and patted him on the back:

- Today you are tired, I don't want you to tell us anything about your story, all you have to do today, champion .. is to eat and wash and go to sleep, tomorrow I will hear from you all about you.

The owner tried to say something, but the king said:

"I don't need to worry about anything, and I will strive to ensure that your son (Sands) is your best companion.

- Exclaimed the prince (Sands), saying:

- After that, my lord ..

The men mentioned did not submit the form c (soma style), but climbed two stairs up to the soma style desired room, and there was also one question:

- See what happened to my comrades after him?

And the answer was when God is one.

* *

Too many days passed for me, and I borrowed strength and borrowed from the prince (Sands) more, and strengthened my relationship with him, and the block knew that they were on the way to war, and did not think, and decided to share with them, and you know the rest ..

So a seal (catfish model) recently and then she exclaimed (Lily) and she smiled in sweetness:

- Thank God you returned to us safe and sound ...

Grab the prince (Sands) by the hand, which silenced her, and angrily looked at him, and shouted in his face, and turned his forehead and reddened cheeks.

- How to catch ...

He pointed to his mouth as she drew everyone's attention to him in surprise, pointed to his ear mark meaning they are heaven, and missed the seconds of silence that interrupted him (Strand) said:

Book of the Damned Episode 11 - Dark Forest
    Taking the prince of the sands is paradise and then asked everyone to shut up
- What do you mean "mine"? ..

The prince whispered (Sands), said:

- I feel that we are not alone, and that something is peeping at us from behind the branches.

Stimulate the file (wisely) and feel the safety of his fist and say:

- Ready if at any time

Take the rest of our heroes into the darkness of the surrounding forest, so that they can see what follows and boils in them, but they could not penetrate into the darkness, and here the king said (to the wise) once again:

- Let's continue our path, but do not give up your desire.

Wavy hearts (Lily) still walk between the owners and do not notice that they have never been the owners of these sparkling eyes, which you follow silently, as if she is waiting for the right moment to attack, and he walks to addresses from branch to branch in Hefei and happy for them.

* * *

Taking (Burgundy) Runs down and chokes with overexertion and tries to escape from the king's soldiers, and from time to time looks back to make sure he was able to escape from them after losing his uncle, and suddenly stops to catch his breath and listen and look at the office around him .. he stood in a place cluttered with trees, ko-trees are large, they even blocked the arrival of the sun on Earth, and every now and then he froze from the sound of a bird, and suddenly he uttered an annoying cry and seemed to be afraid something, and the interaction of its owner with it. And he translated him at a frightening pace and shot with his feet in the wind, and from afar came the voice of the Southern Queen of Darkness after him ..

I took the branches wandering in front of his face and mixed things up in front of his eyes, thinking of nothing but running away from them, he took what he was saying to his enemy and did not notice that he was standing on the edge of a high cliff, and his body falls into the void, he is trying to grab something, then you know that one of the bushes sprouted in the belly of this wound, he looked down and found a river creature .. The crackle of a branch announcing a front weight (burgundy) suggested it was and flutter his heart between his ribs, and during this terrible situation the soldiers approached the edge of the regiment, and they looked down, they were looking, they could find it, but the foliage was hidden from above, and now the retreat of the soldiers leaves this place, and in this the moment the branch crackles quickly and the roar and the personality of its owner quickly fall from such a high height, and take the form ... and broadcast non-stop.

* * *

I took one of the petals of this tree, fell down until it settled on the floor over her sisters, and poured a large amount, and then collapsed under the feet of the horses of our heroes, and they do not care about it, and suddenly I told the queen (sage), and he raised his eyebrows:

- Get ready, it looks like our comrades were already ready to attack !!!

Everyone uses it and they grab onto their weapons, and suddenly the horses threw something back to their front, and she looked confused and she was afraid of something, and the dog tried to control her, tighten the harness, but the horses insisted on their position, and everyone's eyes widened, and the hubbub reigned among all, and then the prince shouted (Sands).):

- Take care of the horses and try to control them.

Already she has adhered to her appearance well, and without much jumping, the animal and the sign (strand) from the horse, which he got on the occasion of the building, and taking each one asks himself what kind of thing it was that knocked him out so quickly !!

Book of the Damned Episode 11 - Dark Forest
        And suddenly black leopards appeared to them
He did not find the answer in himself, but at the moment when the boat carried them to answer, and very quickly also, it turns out that the owner of our (Lily's) something in the dark can be seen with his eyes, the reflecting light is terrible and scary, and now , she said to the king (sage) and refers to this creature .:

- Here he is looking at us!

Look at all the places to go and they found that this pair of eyes was staring at them defiantly and did not waste a second until the back of the other pair of eyes moved away from the first, and then back the other and the other, as if the place was teeming with these. bright eyes, and now the prince said (sands), and he looks around:

- They are all around us ..

He exclaimed (catfish style) and he tightens his horse's bridle, trying to control it:

- Looks like we are in a death trap !!!!

Looking at the dossier (wisely) for the whole situation and thinking, he whispered:

- Why don't they attack now?

She replied (Lily):

- I feel that their leader did not ask them to attack after, they should keep him.

And this pair of sparkling eyes calmly approached them, I accepted the approach of even the puffing personality of the owner to that falling light due to the intertwining of branches, said the King (sage):

- Lord, these are black leopards

Strand exclaimed and lowered himself gently to the ground, holding his horse's fork. :

- Looks like they're going to kill us separately

The king said (wisely) and follows this cheetah and approaches slowly

- Shh, idiot, do not speak and do not move, any movement is now in our doom.

The silence of everyone in anticipation, and he took this black leopard, which is approaching and approaching, and takes the purchase through the nose (strand) And spins around him, then smiles a little and his owner almost dies of fear, and is already shaking with all his cells of horror even the cheetah smiled for him, then the grimace on his fangs and accepting the requests roared high, and then several black panthers appeared, attacking them with incomparable ferocity, and the higher your swords, axes and arrows, claiming their number, but there were many of them, and it was difficult for Max to do this, and the hand of the Black Panther would start hand-to-hand combat because of the number of her large ones, and her teeth, which carry the smell of death ..

* * *

The body of a pigeon (burgundy) In this river, he quickly fell down like a stone, but his master took him in his arms to the right and left until he rose to the surface to inhale air that almost exploded and he almost raised his head, even spit out the water that got into his mouth and inhaled air, and pulled him to look up, and found that the soldiers were looking at him and found him, introduced into the reading the same thing that only minutes and be when, he decided to continue his escape quickly, and did not leave a second to think, but allowed the same current that quickly carried him and carried him away from the place of its fall ..

And while he found the trunk of a huge tree that floated on the surface of the water and settled at the edge of the shore, and gathered around its long reed legs, and quickly came up to it, and hid within it ...

Book of the Damned Episode 11 - Dark Forest
Try the burgundy skin between the stems and leaves of the papyrus
And what if he did it even on the back of the South Queen of Darkness, and they looked, and they did not even notice his place, so they climbed this stem and did not notice how he trembled with fear and his heart beat, learn ... and learn
They tried to look between the stems of the papyrus, and then smile a little, and silence everything except the sound of pouring water, the owner did not achieve his place and waited a minute, it was that there was a lot of sticky stuff crawling all over his body, and what if he felt on there was even a cry of panic on his face, which frightened him, and unfortunately the soldiers did not get a lot, and then one of them said to the other:

- Did you hear that?

- Do not

Quote from the trunk of the tree again and he said first:

- I think I heard, see what !!!

When I feel that it would be him, Wang in his place and held his breath, and felt that his heartbeat would do it, but it did not happen, he said one soldier to another:

- She seems to be one of the birds of the water ..

First shut up and listen to why something is happening, kind of shook his head saying

- Maybe so.!!

Then they left, and they left, and they think he left with them ..

The dude's hat in its place was so convinced that the place was empty, and they are there, and that he almost completely even felt extraordinary freedom, from his place a little and found a gap in the stem, which I did not expect, only in my imagination, let's say into place and he watches this miracle that has landed in the water.

* * *

The signed body of this cheetah also lay motionless on the ground after it was stabbed by one of our heroes in this bloody battle, and on one of the branches there was a creature that watched what was happening in silence, and if we worn out a little , then our opinion is loud and it is clear that there was someone standing there, ready to hammer in its outlines in the darkness of the jungle, and easily the Panthers jumped into the area of easy and clear navigation, navigation clearly or not ... exactly its features!

This strange creature ... a configuration that combines the kingdom of humans and the kingdom of cats, her eyes were clear blue, like the eyes of cats reflect light, and ears too, and the human nose disappeared, and the nose changed, like the noses of a train, and the back tusk in her mouth ..

He was the color of her skin, gray, and he could move her black hair down her back, and her body was graceful, and her claws were in her hands, and he covered the same thing with some kind of fabric that showed off more than you deserved, and I took head to the right and north, and stopped behind the Panthers, and accepted the approach of our heroes in silence, frowning at her terrible fangs ..

- She exclaimed (Lily) and was amazed:

Book of the Damned Episode 11 - Dark Forest
A creature of strange configuration appeared in front of them.
- Lord, is it really true? !!

Received the file (wisely):

- And creates the money you know

- Exclaimed the Prince (Sands):

- See why you stopped the Panthers !!!!

The file answered (wise) and is still available to this creature and approaches them in snobbery is understandable:

- Be sure that this creature controls him in some way ..

Stop this creature in front of them and she put her hand on her thin waist, and I looked at them and as a check, said Don King (sage) reluctantly:

- Peace and mercy of Allah ..

She continued to look at him with wide eyes, repeating safety in apprehension, and a long silence, and she and the prince (sands) said something, but she said in a voice that sounded like alignment:

- You, too.

Surprised that everyone understood (catfish style)

- It's in Arabic !!

An odd tone of voice answered

- And what is not spoken about me in Arabic and I live on Arab soil

- I quietly asked her (Lily). :

- Who are you really?

Everyone shut the fuck up and dominated the food and they thought they wouldn't speak, although curiosity got the better of it and finally said:

- You are now in my kingdom, and you entered there without my permission .. it is actually on the visitor to show yourself first !!

The king bowed (wisely) a little, and understood the meaning of her conversation and said in his Rakhi voice:

- Sorry, madam, for what happened and what is the reason for our losses, stranger, blind and seemingly perspicacious ..

Book of the Damned Episode 11 - Dark Forest
   The progress of the prince, the wise man said to him: believe what caused our losses
Annoyed (Lily) by what the king did was raised his forehead and wandered into the kitchen, where, but the prince (Sands) met the target and is referred to as, quiet reluctantly and almost out of anger, while I took this little creature hovering around the king like a cat that hovers around its owner, and took the open school system discerningly and said:

- You have to upgrade.

- Honestly, I am a Great Merchant in my country and these assistants to me and my friends

I twisted around the door and then said:

- Liar !!

Faded the file and stop talking, and stop breathing only (Lily) I scream:

- How dare you, cat muck?

And he tried to hit her with a sword, but she was lighter and faster, the acrobat encouraged her body to rise into the air and can accompany us from behind, I grabbed her by the head, looked freely and spurred her fears to cover her neck, and since the surprise of the beauty escalated and things went to the extreme .. Yes, it rolled so hard downhill

* * *

I put the (burgundy) cuff on the floor of the chest, which needs to be done, that is, to observe these creatures, which I took to fiddle with water here and there in a childish way, and laughed their fill of this place, and during this meeting one of them on that chest, and began to gradually open her legs and cover them with water, and then asked the other of them to say if they were looking very careful? :

Book of the Damned Episode 12 - New Creatures
The solution is to discover the gorillas and creatures in previous episodes .. it will be a dream come true to buy a starting point for another stranger's creatures.
- Oh, what is it? Is that a mole ?!

Laughed the first childish laugh and she replied saying:

- If this thing with a mole has been in my family since childhood ..

- Can I take a closer look at her? !!

- Of course, why not? there is?

She bent down last to leave this birthmark, and when I did, she suddenly fell like a shock to her friend, saying that she was raising her eyebrows:

- What happened to you?!

She pointed to the chest she was wearing:

- There is someone shooting at me from this trunk ..

And when I heard this word for the first time, I got up from my place on the spot, and everything after I silently looked at this chest in anticipation, even the back of the hands (Burgundy) is out of place after he learned that he leaves from the south, the Queen of Darkness, launched Friday and stepped back from him until he came out completely and looked at them in stern surprise, not like the obviously surprised above !!

We were a group of girls of picturesque beauty, their eyes were blue and wide, and their hair was blond like the Sun behind them, their backs were smooth and clear, their bodies were white and graceful, and the presence of pink, all this was not named to amazement its owner; but all the girls would have a pair of long white wings, as if they were exactly Angels, try to shave some off after you found the place of its owner, but he said he was embarrassed. :

- Hallelujah that reduces money, you know !!

Then he continued his speech, telling the girl that she was sitting at the top of the stem:

- Wait, wait, I don't want to offend anyone ..

Smile with all your boy, refuse to rot, was ready to fly, only that girl with a mole that she curiously told him in her sweet voice:

- What prompted you to stay in this trunk ?! Did you know we were coming? Who sent you? AND....

- He interrupted her, smiling and shaking his head. :

- Calm down, ma'am, I cannot answer all these questions !!

And when she saw the girl, she felt a little safe and started killing her master's son, while Fuller says:

- What pushed me to stay in this place is a long story, a waste of time when you tell everything from ear to ear .. I don't mind, but did you come to a note or not ... this is the first time I visit this place initially, and not my derby buddy in despair, or that it's luck that I came here this time to see you, the girl said, and she tilts her eyebrows to the top:

- It seems that you are the owner of the eloquent language, we humans appreciate people through their dogs, and have earned the trust that entered our hearts ..

He bowed slightly to the owner and whispered:

- Yes, ma'am.

- Raise your head, young man, and do not bow to Allah.

"I was also a mediator of the group mind, the freshness of your voice captivated me to park there, ma'am.

- Do not tell us with yours, but we will tell you about ourselves and the secret of your existence, everyone was thirsty and thirsty and entered my story.

Its owner, and will return the memory back to him, said:

The book of the Damned episode 12 - new creatures
Discover a Burgundy place where beautiful girls had their white wings, even he thought they were angels who fell from the sky.
- History from the very beginning ... was once a long time ago
....

Let's take a piece of history from the book of the damned who chase them, everyone listens to it intently, and never notices those eyes that pursue them in silence, as if these eyes are waiting for the right moment to join them at the right moment.

* * *

He landed (A.J.) on his horse and looked at the mountain that stood at the foot of the base, looked up to the top and said with an accent reminiscent of the groan of a snake:

- Finally, my beloved came to you.

He continued to smile:

- It looks like you will find yourself in my arms, finally ..

And the aspects in the rock quickly approach, and then carry a quiver on their back, and took the wind of manipulation of the lapels, picked up his clothes behind him in the mythical scene, then heading down the mountain, so that he says to climb to reach his goal, and evil is seen in his eyes is terrible for the border.

* * *

Widened eyes (Lily) in horror, a glance at the dangers of these feline-people, who were ideally positioned on her neck and stood motionless and motionless, as if she was afraid to indulge these claws in the first movement of it in her veins, and the nave (catfish model) and (the staff of) freedom Automatic would do nothing of them to set them up; but the king (sage) stopped them with his hand, while that feline-human laugh-like alignment said:

"I don't think anyone is stupid enough to drag him into this business and make me and the leopard people, who love the smell of warm blood and fresh meat, as their prey !!

The edge of the file (wise) is trying to control the position .. - he asked, coming closer to them:

"We don't want anything from you all, ignoring your people .. all we want is to get through safely.

She looked at him, a sudden insight made him stop in his place, said a tone carrying a resonant frequency:

- But I want it ...

I took it, surprising everyone with its frequency, this is it! He took the file (wise) this opportunity and said quickly:

- We obey you ..

I laughed that the cat was human again, and said mockingly:

- Are you used to always lying?

- What do you mean?

- Can't you see that I smell lies and pictures !! I am good at rebooting.

The king disappeared, and the prince (Sands) exclaimed quickly:

- Believe me, sir, it's true, because dogs and cats are able to smell your fear ... and through it enjoy the discrimination between truth and falsehood ..

He told (Strand) in a hoarse voice that they would see the world on her face. :

- And who are you, the creature is standing ------

Laughter is a mixed-signal laughter to harmonize the sector, indicating that it refers to the neck (Lily), which took over the stage:

- Will you never learn your lesson ?!

The leopards growled and immediately announced their anger, and then the prince (Sands) said, trying to play the position a little with a smile:

- In fact, we are from different places and we all strive for the same goal ..

Here is the file (wise) exclaimed the same thing, quickly forget even this is his lie:

- Although we will help you in your endeavor, what do you want?

Then hem a little and move closer to the words:

- Leave this innocent child so we can help you all ..

And when I heard (Lily) the word "baby", she got angry and decided to apply some of the charm I had learned, she said angrily and frowned.

- What do you have in mind?

Smile (catfish model) in sheer gloating as the king said again:

- You, my baby ..

The dilated pupils of her eyes screamed saying:

- You yourself are to blame, I will teach you a lesson that you will not forget ....

The silence suddenly became such as if she did not want to expose him, and then after I took it, muttering unintelligible words, then inhaled from the other side far away and it was only a matter of a few seconds that even stuck to his lips, and he tried to open his mouth, but to no avail, and she saw a human cat, what happened here, she said in a rage:

- So you are a witch !!!

She (Lily) in everything:

- Are you afraid of me?

- I'm not afraid of anyone but God.

I then followed the feline human speech, addressing the king with the words:

- Return it to its natural state ..

She (Lily) exclaimed quickly. :

- What do you care?

The book of the Damned episode 12 - new creatures
The kitten will die .. The queen of cats ..
And then I feel like a prince (sands) that things will be believed more, so to speak:

- We must achieve a solution to the satisfaction of all parties at the same time.

- She (Lily) exclaimed to add something, but the latter interrupted her, quickly saying:

- I do not want any demands - this is not a simple demand, walking calmly through my forest in an interview.

Here she (Lily) exclaimed, and she is still in the arms of this creature:

- We will not achieve any demands ... but a year from these forests at least turn your nose ...

Hemet is a creature to them, but to the right of her is the prince (sands) in another attempt to control the position:

- (Lilia) please help me, the employee will not guess the impudence, please think about it carefully ..

Be silent a little while the subordinate says:

- First, bring your (wise) state back to normal.

I thought a little, and then sighed as if she recognized her master and muttered a few words, and then the king returned to his business, subordinate to the prince (Sands), said::

"I was thinking about the first node, this is the role of you, ma'am, so that we can help you all, and our friend, she did nothing to you.

We camped on beautiful bird pictures, and everyone thought that they would never leave her and would focus their risks at any moment on the neck (lily), and ....

If everyone thought and pushed him away from their chest and there she cried (Lily):

- Now I can avenge you, life .....

Interrupted by the king, he put his fingertips to her lips, squeezed them tightly, and she frantically tried to free herself from him, saying to him, smiling with sweetness:

- Forgive them, please ... these are always funny problems, and then we want to know your story in order to achieve what you ask ...

I didn't add the creation time, as if she was expecting it, she said majestically, with pride, and she lifts her nose high with her voice, which combines the sounds of humans and cats:

- My name is Princess (the kitten will die.) .. a descendant of the great kings of this jungle.

I laughed (Lily), cynically said:

- Really ?!

I looked at her (the kitten will die) and the prince told her in anger (Sands):

- Keep your word, please, we are all thirsty and curious to know who you are ??

Showing the owner, we said:

- Do not disturb me ..

You can't (Lily) tweet it quietly to her about it when referenced by the word (these) in a defensive tone like:

- You mean me when I tell you it's a kitten?

He told him (the sage) and saw in her eyes:

- Easy, all my ... easy everything and we will get used to ..

No one then knew anything ... and she (the kitten dies), she returns with her memory of the distant past:

"All I know is a Horde of demi-humans, half-cats, I don't know exactly where we came from! So tell me one of the first ever, but all I know is that we did not value living with people ever, that we settled here in this great forest, and see the Starfish as not our kingdom, hidden from people's eyes? inside? Over time, he became a king and workers there, and the end, and our king, but not enemies in the forest, and we do not know where they came from and how they appeared ?! It's strange that they are half human, half dog! They were a group of savages, don't look between them as if they were mercenaries, they mean nothing, only support him, they attacked our kingdom a lot and no one could stop them. they took the best of you and our children, and one day she told my father that one is free in our kingdom, he should plant your daughter ... and do not return to her only after many months ... inevitable, and actually smiled to me that his nanny and I have been in one of the mountains for almost a year, and when we returned, we did not find anyone in the kingdom !! Only palaces and houses are shapeless and lifeless, and no one knows why ... where did they go ?!

The question confused me very much, and we waited for the return of any person, but there was no one since the time when my nanny died and I was left alone, and I was able to tell people in any sector that this panther was always in my service.

Book of the damned episode 12 - new creatures
Half human, half dog .. they are very powerful people and it is difficult to defeat them .. and they are detained for having their own bird people stole their kitten to die ..
Having finished his story, the prince exclaimed (sands), saying to him with ardor:

- Poludog, what is their fate?

- They are still alive, and they attacked them and stole something dear from me, we were able to escape from them. Me and his nanny before we die.

- How much is this thing?

She answered, she said:

"That's what I want you to take from them and bring it to me.

She (Lily) in satire:

- What is it, being late for the train?

She answered as if she had received a bomb:

- This is a great call .....

A period of silence, and then she suddenly said:

- It's a bird people !!

And then silence fell on everyone ..

* * *

Suddenly, during a conversation (Burgundy), a dog barking is heard, coming from afar, and the ticket is the dog that was with him, he lost during his escape, and before that, what happens to the shares in the trunk, which was located above him! ! The shuttlecock leaped from its place, and the winged girls screamed about this and that, and hit the air, flying into space, and their owner was a push, he looked at the owner of the arrow, and quickly found that they were shooting at him south of the queen of darkness with another arrow, he could not move, as if he was proving his place with nails, and shot an arrow from his side with frightening speed and eyes ... and suddenly felt that something was lifting him from the ground !! And above, they found two of them flying in space, and they threw arrows to play out, the situation was difficult for everyone.

* * *

- A bird like no other !!

He said (the kitten will die), and she sits on this stone in front of our heroes, and they listen to him in silence, after they sat on these stones, they are also scattered everywhere, some in the forest, and then the queen (sage) shouted::

- And where is this bird?

Intervention (Lily) told him::

- Wait a bit .. we have not yet found out what kind of bird it is ..

Asked (a lock) who raises D.'s eyebrows saying:

- And what is this bird?

Answer (Leila) said:

- I know him well !!

The silence was a little to include some importance in her conversation was:

- This is a giant bird with the head of a giant eagle, and the body of a lion, mighty, South Sudan, the air is frightening up to the neck, the tail of a bull, the sides of the wings make them fly by the material when they fly in the air and he does not need it, because he is bewitched and unique, and ordered by one single owner, and to ride it on someone else, it is difficult to tame.

- exclaimed the prince (Sands), which surprised me. :

- What a bird, fantastic !!

Said that the king (sage) directed his speech to (the kitten).):

- How do we get it ?!

- I'll go with you, you don't know the way ..

A sigh (catfish style) said:

- How is it better than going alone?

Look (Lily) think hard and exclaim, they look into her eyes, saying:

- Oh wait, this cat is hiding something important on them!

She said (the kitten will die) sarcastically:

- How do you know?!

But she has her back to him. :

- Oh, I forgot that you are a demon ..

Look at this buddy, We said:

- Forget this disappointed conversation and tell them what you have .. or you tell them that I just

There was a silence, and everyone looked at the fact (hotly) that I threw a fierce look at our friend, here is the dossier (wisely):

- What's there ?!

She replied (Lily) in anger:

- Ask the cats what else is there?

Two seconds in silence, then she said (the kitten dies), and then in a low voice, she carries a melancholic tone:

- No one walks in front of them for the jumper and does not return after that !!

And stop the news in Thunderbolt's ears just like the last time, did they look at some, here she (Lily) exclaimed at the level of what happened:

- Ha ... What do you think now? So are we going to catch him ?!

Or answer one of them as if they were a bunch of statues muted by a chorus.

* * *

He offered to fly girls B (burgundy) from the forest with tall trees and a huge number of twigs to a place, so his owner said:

- Where are you taking me?

- One of the girls answered:

- To our house ..

- Where exactly is he located? to?

- Like this ..

- Where to???

- You will see ... don't be so impatient ..

And he quickly landed inside this forest, where suitable marvelous intertwined trees hanging on branches appeared, hanging wooden bridges were called together, and the whole house in front of him was a large balcony.

There were a lot of half-these girls of different ages .. men ..
women ... elderly .. children whose wings withered, the largest of
them over time, and babies did not grow wings after going into the
courtyard of the largest house girls have landed in the world, lead
their master, who rolls gently, then stops and looks around in
surprise, and then says:

- Where exactly are we?

- answered one of the girls, passing in front of him. :

- You are now in a nursing home ..

- Who are you?!

She turned to him and said with blue eyes::

- I'm going ... take your time ..

Book of the Damned Episode 12 - New Creatures
I did not grow wings for the small bird kingdom because of the
small age, while the older ones have faded wings ..
Suddenly a huge door opened in front of her, exquisite carving, a
pattern of birds with a human appearance, and they seem to be
talking about what, but her owner is indecisive, and when he
entered, until his eyes widened, the country does not appear from
the outside from the inside, it is huge in height , and its roof is
decorated with the most wonderful inscriptions, and in the roof
there is also a glass dome of great beauty, and everywhere there
were pots with fragrant flowers, and birds of different shapes and
colors come and go in this place in a contented state, big behind,
and people stand and the guards, dressed in leather, bright colors,
and one of the girl's maids quietly suggested, she said that her tone
carried the wound with concern clearly:

- Where have you been, princess (Dove)? Your father the king was worried about him, so he almost sent the knights of the kingdom to look for you.

- And here I am in front of you in perfect order.

Stop (Burgundy) shouted at her advisor:

- You're a princess, aren't you ?!

- What happened to you?!!

He slapped himself on the palms, smiled and said:

- How could I not know that from the very beginning there are girls around you?

Then she went up to him and one of the maids said:

"My lady, the queen knew that you were coming and asks for your presence with him ..

Buddy (tan) fast:

- I'll tell you something, you go to the file, and I'll activate them ..

Then he quickly turned to go out and stop at the door, and remembered that he was high in rubbish and had no way to burn, went puzzled, and then returned to the princess (dove) and approached her ear and whispered::

- Did I tell you anything else ?!

She put her hands on her waist and smiled with the corner of her mouth that looked like beads said to cherry:

- Ha ...

- Come with me to drop me off ..

She shook her head to Crane, he was on his own, not giving out his voice and he glared at her:

- Eh, son Sparrow, if I could, I would pluck your feathers thrown here.

Then Hem says in a clear voice:

- And now?!

I grabbed his hand and told them not to enter the palace. :

- First we will see my father, not my story, and maybe it will help you ..

And in order to stop before the king, sitting on a huge throne, decorated with red gold, which is for, and to receive the dignity that his two birds had, the individual stands behind him, which gave him a bone above his greatness, which came from his bizarre and huge beard, and his eyes are clear blue, and this blue tattoo, which occupied most of his face, so he asked after the tanned dude in a whisper:

"Weren't his wings different ?!

- She said barely audibly. :

- How can kings in our kingdom have their wings dyed black, unlike the rest of their hair, and then bow down before him right away, before he kills you right away ..

He bowed to his master immediately after the King said in a rough voice:

- Where have you been, (dove) is there? And why did you put this creature between us ?! Have you forgotten the laws of our kingdom?

She said to her slave:

- Listen, your story, Your Majesty will free them from everything.

The king raised his hand to his chin, slid back and spent a few seconds, as if thinking, and then suddenly said:

- Then sit next to me ..

Then he continued, pointing to his master:

- And you, a human being .. tell us your story, but leave me until I understand what I am guided by and learn, and from the very beginning ..

A sigh, its owner took a deep breath, then took a chunk of his story from the beginning and aroused keen interest.
Opening this rock, when Seth (A.J.) introduced him to her, he ascended to the surface of the mountain and, taking a falling from a great height, falling quickly terrifyingly down, looked at her and began to follow her gaze until she disappeared from his field of vision , said sarcastically:

- "If I fall, it will be a terrible fall!"

Then he swallowed and took the continuation of his ascent to the top, he continued, shaking his head:

- "What a fall!"

And in the field of vision, almost the sun changed, and, seeing the structure of trees from the top of a distant slope, he said to himself:

"Looks like (A.J.) you'll stay here overnight and continue tomorrow."

And the owner entered one of the hollows and buried his nose to spend the night and continue in the morning,

Yes, will follow his path to reach the book of the damned.

* *

- The Queen shouted in the south in a rage .:

- "Run !!!"

Then she resolutely continued and began to shout at them insanely clear:

- "As you say?! "

One of the soldiers said that it was he who stood up in fear of them:

"It's a starry night now, madam."

Exclaimed:

"No, it looks like this fight will save you."

The book of the Damned episode 13 The final steps

The wrath of the queen of darkness and conquered the south because of their
The loyal soldiers said in awe:

"But ma'am ..."

He did not finish, because she interrupted him, saying:

"Now you will pay for this neglect of the body!" "

Then raise the plane to the sky, which rattled aggressively, to the energy of guilt, which in the upper plane was brutally attacked by the light until it entered a trance of light, the eyes and heard the beautiful sound of the screams of the tortured, as if coming from hell! And it lasts a long time, and then everything stops, the light immediately dims, and the soldiers lie on the ground with their faces down, and everyone sees them and thinks that they are dead bodies, just a movement of the weak chest of one of them! Then the third and fourth, until they moved from their place, the rest all spoke in turn, they looked at themselves, not believing that they were still alive, and one at the other in attacks of severe panic! After that, they looked at each other, even took turns immediately turning their faces and they looked at their hands, I mean ..

Their concern !! So they shouted after her in confusion even more than the first time, she turned everyone into freaks, amazing shape! Here I took a folder with the inscription:

- "These are kicks as if following an order to me."

Then she continued:

- Let's finish our journey, we came to a lot of what we wanted, and nothing happened. really take care of him. "

And then she walked in front of the army and laughed like a demon that came out of hell.

* * *

Kark this bird, flying away from this silence, which fell on the file (wise), is with him, and suddenly a piece of this photo says::

- "I will go with you, but I hope for an illustration."

She said (the kitten will die):

- I'm going to tell you everything.

She (Lily) exclaimed cynically. :

- "All ears to you, cat lady."

I looked at her (the kitten would die) was turned on if the shell in her fangs and claws would rid her of them; but she fell to her site which said:

"I went with the others before that to try and get the bird back, they were passing by the forest, but we didn't use the recovery jumper and they couldn't return."

She (Lily) is clear in her sarcasm:

- "Why ?!"

She replied (the kitten will die):

- Because, perhaps, in the cowardice of these people or in the incorrect fulfillment of the agreed plan, they ended up in a forbidden zone, unpacking the precious life of their person and a path fraught with risk. "

Exclaimed (sage):

- For example?

- "The road there is not easy, there is the next one behind the trees"

- exclaimed (catfish model) in amazement:

- "Trees are a killer ?!"

- Yes, the trees speak and all the passages next to him! There is a legend that says that in ancient times there was a city of working people in agriculture and to have cows under their supervision, and one day they woke up and they did not find their cows, only one family was left with the war as it is .. They thought that they are shoplifters or their hand in the disappearance of the cows, collect the villagers and this family to death, bind them in these trees and leave them to die, the legend says that after death they lived their lives in these trees and they returned to take revenge from the people of this village and killed everyone who passes in front of them, his sentence or the rest of them, and they decided to cut down these trees, but they did not work, they never, and so they left this place it became a deserted highway does not pass alone and then never ...

He said (Strand):

- "What a wonderful thing!"

Spoken by (Leila):

- What else is there? "

The book of the Damned episode 13 The final steps
They took their lives in the trees and returned to take revenge.
- "There is nothing else to hide a non-lock is considered doggy style
for this sex. Then take a jumper."

Then the prince (Sands) intervened, saying:

- And what will happen after that? "

I looked at him and said:

"I will help you, as promised, get out of here."

- Our friend exclaimed.

- And if we help you, what will happen? "

She answered (True) with a challenge:

- "I will leave the Tatars face to face in the jungle forever ... so come
out of someone alive, never!"

Having said about this conversation even so that everyone silently
looked at each other as if they were fighting during their silence,
here is the file (wise):

- I will help you, no matter what.

He had a half smile on his lips (the kitten will die), while the murder
(Leila) said:

- "(Wisely) ... you want us to suffer."

- "But keeping safe."

- "Think carefully, (wise), she can never outlive one of them, and will never benefit the bird."

"But we will create God with the bird, and God's help with us."

Looking to (the kitten died) tell him:

- Come on, show us the way, and let's not waste time. "

Silence (lilies) silence about dissatisfaction and our hero follows its consideration, namely, on Friday, after saddling horses with horns that adorn their foreheads, and took (kitten dies) to jump from branch to branch and tree to another, and everyone follows her in silence into the forest ...

Dark forest .

* * *

It is dark in this forest of tall trees that stood on the branches of the houses of the minif's palace, when we approach a little to the palace we see that (wine) has already finished its story, the king of birds said:

- "What a wonderful tale, however, is not over yet"

The king was silent for a moment and rubbed his chin.

- Listen, son, I would do you any help so that you can get the book, but what a trick with the hand; I have all I can do is allow you to have the period that you want, you will be here whatever you want and if you like the course and I want to live with us. we assured you that if you want to go one day, we highly recommend you supplies for and one of our guards to go wherever you go. "

The owner's smile and the hem of the dress:

- Thank you, sir, for the service.

First smile he said:

- "Solved easily and simply in the kingdom of birds"

Then he indicated that he was accompanied by one of the guards and took him to his room, leaving behind his princess (dove) with her father, who approached him and said:

- Father, I want to help him until he gets the book and returns to his sister? "

The book of the Damned episode 13 The final steps
Allowed filenames that inhabit the bird kingdom the way he likes
The king got up from his throne and went to the window of the palace, and shaved in the dark to set up camp on Lesnoy, only a few dim lights extending from this house to the trees, he said, thinking:

- "My daughter (dove), you know that we have been living in isolation from the world since ancient times! We do not disagree with the rest of the peoples of the other world, and I will tell him if you do not know him ..

The silence of the king, carried by his thoughts into the distant past and early times in the kingdom, he continued:

- They were all people from one, but there were some other mutations that made them different forms of people, and this mutation of rejection of ordinary human beings became the owners of these untouchable mutations, which he had so senior that he was born like any ordinary a child who, over the course of days, has grown wings and claws like a bird! Dim and his mother sailed into the woods, got up and became young people, his father died as Mulder knew no one other than his reputation and showing it off, and decided to visit him after his mother died, but he was rejected under pressure and samples of his feathers were ripped out ! And then he returned to the forest, burdened with wounds, he was helped by a girl from the village, who took pity on him, because he was so handsome .. he had golden hair and clear blue eyes .. and his skin is white .. his body is slender, and In the event of severe exhaustion, here the girl left her family so that he would not fall in love, his house was hidden from view, the girl's parents said they were looking everywhere, could never find him, and one day they returned to them. she was very worried about her pregnancy, and helped her mother get up and get tested (a girl and two boys). And over time, the boy's wings grew, and the girl had a normal son! Spread this news, and threaten the mother's care for her cubs in the forest, and prove to the people of the village and the burning period, and what this girl and her children will bring, like the devil's campaign, and the flight of a young winged with her family, but the wife died of weight fatigue and stress, and after the child's trip, the natural child remained both winged and flew to their father above the trees and made them beta, and over time the family expanded into a tribe, and then the people populated the trees and created the people, and then became the great kingdom of living beings . in the treetops, and we are the same today. A kingdom of the forgotten, the missing, knowing no one and not wanting to know, and I think it's wise to keep it a secret so that we can keep our existence in peace among the trees. "

The silence of the king is a little spoken (little Dove):

"But, my father, he changed course, and maybe he will accept us humans right now."

The king of birds said without meeting his gaze:

"My child, little people are enemies of the unknown ... and they initially do not know about us."

- The princess said, putting her hand on her father's back and trying to look into his face:

"But I can see it by the fact that we are helping this young man; he strives for the thread "

He turned to her father and she gently shook her head.

- "(Dove), I am still young to make judgments about the things that happen around you, everything requires wisdom and experience and a look into the future, I beg you to make your mind always be the government, and not your emotions, child my."

I tried the princess (dove) to ask her father, saying:

- "Dad, it's true that I'm still small, but I understand that the company is good."

The king's almost patience is fulfilled, and he says:

- "(Dove) .. the words of another in this thread will not accept him."

Then the silence continued as he looked into her clear blue eyes. :

- Then I see everyone's interest, and I think it's better not to involve yourself in what we are irreplaceable in. "

Here a kiss was imprinted on her cheek and said:

- Please leave all this to me, go to your room, sleep well and do not worry about anything, and I will do everything in my power.

She looked her father in the eyes for a long time, and then said:

"You see, Father, please."

Then I left him at the same time as something else you are doing, take the file available to her until he disappeared from his field of vision ... out and he turned to look out the window and looked at the lights appearing from the windows of the respective houses, and was surprised:

- "Look what you get in the coming days for (tan) it?"

* * *

The stars shone in the sky like pearls on the Black bed, the Moon that took over pulled the sky, and below there was a dark army, actively moving forward, so that the iron stopped everyone in amazement to stop the revolution, Samir (CEO) is the voice of the queen of darkness in his head said::

- I see that we will stay here overnight, and in the morning we will continue our journey.

The (SEO) point of view of the queen, how she is silent .. the human head screamed in the affirmative in the voice of a strong entity, like the roar of a powerful waterfall:

- "Very much here tonight."

And so that the soldiers would hear that they quickly set up camp and set fire to, they set up a large tent that the queen in the pride entered, and everyone outside was waiting for her orders and a long wait ...

Even accepting sleepiness, he inserted his eyelids to the beauty, and the placebo (CEO) in front of people wrapped his body with a piece of cotton to cover it completely, while the veil (Cohen) sank into a deep sleep and began to snore loudly, like the music of Africa, suddenly the silence of the latter came and opening his eyes as if he had not slept, he said, standing at the height of activity! Casting a glance at the owner, who had put his body to sleep, and hearing in his head the voice of the king, who turned to him, he said softly:

- "Yesaaaaaaaaaaaaaaaa"

Gather his clothes and drag them lightly, like a thief, until he got to the tent of his queen and entered her from behind, so that no one else could see, and so that she could see, so I smiled and said to him:

- I miss your nectar, My queen.

Then he threw his body into the boudoir between her and the outside world took a wolf howl and

Endless .

* *

I heard (ja) the sound of wolves howling filled the lower part of the front, which sounds scary, so grab it yourself and try to sleep, and indeed, after a long period of struggle with sleep until another fact is missed, and this thing is called clicking in silence! As if Fahad approached his victim, and then lifted his tail up and decided to sting the sleeping victim!

* *

The stitches (kitten dies) of clutch in this branch are connected with the fact that after almost losing her balance, she followed all, even full trees standing on the edge of the road, and the King (sage) who approached was surprised:

- "Why did you stop ?!"

She (Lily) exclaimed before answering first. :

- Because we are planting trees in front of Cairo. "

The prince said (The Sands):

- "It's true?! "

- "Yes "

He said (Strand):

- "Do it now? How are we going to do it?"

File exclaimed (wise) wondering:

- Is there another way? "

He shook (the kitten will die) his head, and then he (catfish style):

- "And gave him one?"

My baby (Lily) put on a crooked smile over his mouth:

- "Never, never pass one of these trees."

Everyone shut up to hell ... it was amazing, and the Moon, creeping from behind the branches, seemed to illuminate the road in front of them, and then the king said:

- "And you (the kitten will die) how do you exercise it?"

- "Order from above branches"

- "Like this?! "

- "I'll show you "

Then he jumped over the branches to open up, approached the branches and I began to catch him, but he jumped from branch to branch with speed and ease, ran away from the trees and disappeared from his eyes, and soon the pandemonium returned among the branches of the trees, which moved in all directions like long arms, and the owner spoke to her again, smiling. :

- What do you think? "

- Shouted the Prince (Sands):

- Amazing in all respects!

Here I feel, as if for the first time, that his heart is beating wildly, like a little rabbit jumping between his ribs, and I looked into her eyes, at the green steps and drew an oval in the silence of two, and watched her turn and answer them, but he I didn't hear anything, it was the last loneliness in the valley, and looked at him, he smiles sweetly, but (a strand), as it were, slightly on his side, he concentrated, said that he was surprised:

- Did I miss something? "

She (Lily):

- "Obviously you weren't here, this one."

- "I ! "

The King said addressing him his conversation:

- I was waiting for your answer, Amir. "

- "In that? "

She (Lily) in satire:

"I didn't hear anything guys ... excuse him."

The Prince (The Sands), who says:

- What do I hear? "

He looked at the file (wise) silently, but they finish it and he raises an eyebrow. :

- Did I miss something? "

Exclaimed (model catfish) in response to the question:

- "Yes, a lot !!"

After the file (wisely) calmly:

"I would love to know your opinion on how we will die among the trees next time."

"Sorry, buddy, but I wasn't a common sight for you from the beginning."

I laughed (Lily) another exclaimed:

"Didn't I tell you that he was not with us?"

Smile at the dossier (wisely), he said stoically, as usual:

- "Well, prince, the plan is as follows, since (the kitten will die) you can walk among the trees, we will conclude that the Tiger is from him anyway"

- How so? "

- Take your time .. I'll explain everything to you, you have to jump (the kitten will die) on t ...

Beria explains to everyone his plan and goes in transit between the trees next, and everyone called him with obvious interest, and then they went their own way to these trees, until they stood in front of her and looked at her in silence, she smelled of fear, and they felt, that these trees speak to my commute, and suddenly pieces of the file (wise) this voice screams at them, saying::

- "Now "

After that, I heard how (the kitten dies) even jumped on the branches of these trees, which move quickly, like the Hands of an octopus, moving all over the place, trying to catch this creature,

Then the King (sage) said with the same force:

- "Now "

And the White horses to the heart of the trees, penetrating the road quickly, and they ask for the shouts of the riders, and the branches in all directions, because they will not succeed, never, and the arrow quickly launches a branch towards the shoulder (Leela) of creation, namely: the end of the Good Earth !

Take the approaching

AND..

* *

Their princess (dove) that branch in front of the window of the room that lay (tan) and touched it tenderly, the caring owner, opening it, was surprised himself, leaving them:

- (Dove)!

I looked left and right as if afraid to be noticed and whispered until I dropped:

- "Shhhh, let's discuss ... speak more quietly."

"Did I lower my voice? And what brings you here at this late hour of the night ?!"

- We will take care of everything !! "

He bulged his eyes and said out loud:

- What?! "

She quickly put her hand to his lips and whispered:

- "Speak quietly, we will miss you."

I heard the words and whispered:

- "How can we run away, and I'm here, in this high place ?!"

- "No ... nothing, I brought you a surprise!"

Then he looked up and continued:

- "Zarya suggested that requests be sought for everyone in the near future, we need to hurry, I risk my life for you, do not waste time."

I didn't think the owner was strong, and only for seconds he stood on that branch in front of the window, and there she said to him:

- Do you trust me? "

- "Self confidence "

Having said that the pay is to fall from above like a stone! Before giving out any reaction, he felt that he had stumbled
upon something soft, and soon began to tremble in the air, and he was no longer carried ... it's a giant eagle! More than any bird that he saw in his life, and then he took the flying princess (dove) quite simply, this is far away he is behind the lightning .. take the disk of the sun appears in shame announcing the beginning of a new day and new events.

* *

Suddenly, he found the Messenger of Allah himself in a dark cave, from somewhere only a faint reflection of light emanated, and without any preamble he found before him the book of the damned! Now his eyes opened wide and no longer believed the same, but the confusion of his dreams grew, and his hand suddenly grabbed the book, but the discovered hand of another with green scales caught him and disappeared into the darkness !! Then she quickly came back to put on his neck and took thinking hard, I try to enjoy them, but I feel that he is gasping for breath, I can't breathe, moments And ... that's what I thought , and suddenly ...

The book of the Damned episode 13 The final steps
There are some mutants burn the book
Wake up from sleep! Was there something scary waiting for him, and is the owner of the sound that clicks next to him, this is a huge Scorpio! He is the master of the undisputed Scorpions, unless the Scorpio stings him in the tail! Lol, he moved quickly, and did not like to talk about this Scorpio, who resented him so much, and attacked the Messenger of Allah (s) with all his strength and perseverance, I took stones Flying back and forth, and did not surrender to the owner, did not bridle him Scorpio's persistence and thought about what is reported about the tail next .. and a description for the latter! And quickly jumped in front of Scorpio, who chuckled about being the prey of his brave and stopped the attack as if he hadn't made sure his prey didn't run away from him as usual. He enjoys this game so much that before serving them and the insides of your stomach, crackling, they tried to bite him in the tail, but he escaped them simply, and tried Scorpio again, again, again ... and his master was simply got rid of, and all of a sudden everything stopped ... as if there is something preventing Scorpio from continuing to fight! He released the development of back pain from crackling, and then smiled and suddenly disappeared into the darkness, sighed (AJ) with relief and said:

- I thought it was the end, inevitable! "

Silence and hand at the cave entrance follow the sunrise, he continued:

- "If not for some magic that I learned to kill this terrible monster in a few seconds."

Taking the light of the sun making its way into the valley, taking its owner, follow the valley from the summit, which will guide itself through wishful thinking suggested from his dream ... but hey ..

"I saw him .. yes, he did."

The book is guarded by a monster !!

Can you wait on you with his magic and get the book from?

Leaving the question unanswered, watch how the sound of a parrot in space is not interrupted .. the answer was scary to the extreme! Contact point last

The sun shone, and threw a lot of gold over the helmets of the army of darkness, took everyone who was preparing to continue on their way, and then sent them to their queen to continue on their way, and then the beetle sounded with trumpets, drums sounded, banners rose to my sound vibrating from wind, and while he was the leader (CEO), thinking about business, he remembers beyond the bounds his wife and sons, and his home, and then the memory of his fantasy of finding himself a little boy in the workshop of his father, a grieving (swordsman), and father teaches him how to be straight and strong did not disappoint his blade ever.

And then comes what he is taught to ride, equestrian things, then it turns out that he married his cousin on Friday in a simple ceremony, and then his father dies and sadness prevails in his workshop ... I bless my three children, my dying uncle and the presence of the queen between her arms, I go to her to tell him that she heard a lot about this and join his army, I refuse on the grounds that the blacksmith is simple, and I leave the palace, and suddenly I turn over something to quickly let the stairs in front of me, my heart is beating wildly, and I feel anxiety, I stop a little lost, I feel that there is a strong hand, I think: his heart is cruel.

Fell down the stairs and stood in front of this thing, is it a ball of hair or do they have a head for what the owner feels for a long time, almost to walk and walk past him, but he hesitated, as if something pulled him to see what it was?

Bent over to see what this thing is? It was then that his heart began to engage between his legs, and every cell shook in him, and he could not believe his eyes that it was the head of his son who cried out loudly:

- I'm not soooo ...

And he quickly left the stage to find himself in front of the Queen of Darkness, he cries and is exhausted and not from grief:

"I agree, ma'am.

I feel a smile appear on her face, and there this scene slowly disappears, and everyone finds that they are walking, but they stop, and far and within sight of a mountain top appears, on which is the world book of the damned.

So you ran away from the queen in delight, she said when she shouted in her army:

- Now, brave men, we are finally close to our goal, and only a little separates us from him, so not everyone relaxes, but uses, that is, we get what we came for, and we believe in his kingdom, and we are proud of our courage , and by its strength

Book of the damned episode 14 .. contact point last

- The Queen of Darkness cried, - I said, - forward!
K (CEO) hates it, but he was so afraid of her and loved his family more than anything else, and he thought he was running away most of the time, but he was afraid to take revenge on her. and----

I heard her shrill cry:

- To Aaaaaaaaaaaa

Then he raised his scepter to the sky, saw the sun and spread out a black cloud, which took over creeping, green meadows, rocks and forests, and the defense of the army they took the blows to the ground firmly, as the earthquakes cost under their feet, and they continued to walk, but stopped and a cloud of black creeping clouds fell to the ground.

And it stopped

* * *

What if this branch Linda (Lily), until I catch him (the kitten dies), peeks quickly and breaks her violently, we first look between the branch and the last one, the employee already brought in will not say a word, and her silence is here will break his last by saying:

- Don't mention it.

Wide-open eyes (Lily), strangely, quickly, fell from the horse and launched her hand with a sword (the kitten will die), which was scared of the reaction, tilted her head to the right, avoiding the Flying Sword, dividing one of the branches that was heading towards her neck, the smile of the latter said::

- Now we are quits.

Cooperation, these two quickly and then continued to fight, and this is not the end, it has long been their conflict with these branches the following, and during this conflict everyone heard the sound of the file (wise) shouting at them:

- Have they been through

Book of the damned episode 14 .. contact point last
And suddenly the time of branches from under the ground
Having already got down to business, everyone is desperately fighting, and suddenly the vines stopped attacking, and they all turn their weapons in all directions, but (the kitten will die) shout to them, saying:

- Hun - - - - Hon

Everyone stopped and looked at some, whose breath you get from the overabundance of their efforts, while I follow them saying::

"It's over and we got out unscathed.

Smile at everyone as if they are not bumper investigators they have succeeded in but haven't worked in others, and comment out the file (wisely) by saying::

- It's a good fight.

Shook (Lily) (the kitten will die) she put on a big smile and said:

- Welcome, (the kitten dies.)

Then the prince commented (Sands):

- No need to waste more time, come on, use your bird time is running out.

Exclaimed (true):

- You're right, let's continue our journey.

After a little pause, she continued to walk in front of them, and a surprising persistent expression appeared in her eyes. :

- We have a new conflict of a different kind.

The one who followed them (Lily) was, as it were, the best that awaits them:

- Yes, to be honest, with half a floor

They walked all heading into the depths of the jungle and they all hoped to wait for their enemy next and ----

Burn the bird people

Yes all hope

And they never knew that in the future something more awaits them than terrible events.

* * *

Catching (Burgundy) Brescia, the lord of women ascended sky-high, and mistook the patrol of the organization for a forest descending to the bottom, and accepted the change little by little from her sight.

Then the scene changed and, taking a fly between the mountains of white clouds and the disk of the Sun, a light appears on the horizon, soft, and he himself, like in a mythical scene, he loses his arms and tries to touch the clouds, a cry of joy is heard around him, and suddenly it turns out that he is fast descends to the bottom, and took women playing with his hair. strong

The piece, which firmly clings to the feathers of a giant eagle, is about the land of the eagle so much that the surface of this lake either winds, then rises back to the sky, and while it appeared (dove) and stands like a light fly next to the eagle, and taking what was perceived (burgundy), you have to paint a smile on his face, shouting::

- Where are we going to shoot?

Recorded ..

Taking the Eagle, who landed in this tree-free area in the middle of the dense jungle, and filled its wings and took a sound annoying, as he looked up into the sky, so I went down (dove) and stood on the floor, and the owner who landed exclaimed::

- Where are we, (Dove) is?

She replied that she was looking at:

- We in the dark forest offered us the very front that they control about.

His eyes widened uncertified said::

"We ran away from your father and we don't know what he will do when he finds out that we have left.

- Don't wear it my father, I'll be back after you get the book

Taking a bath leads to the heart of its owner, and he told her to the world, looking into her eyes:

- If you don't have to waste any more time and go to the front

And already the Eagle flew over him, his master, and next to them there was (a dove) from afar, I took the sun glare in muted shame, as fear that appeared to portend the coming of a new day or a new war of a different kind

* * *

- There is a castle !!!

He spoke these words (the kitten is dying) and she turns to the ruins of the castle, which still keeps some of its towers listed and high, and everyone noticed that there was an unusual movement, different forms of life appeared, and, puzzling others, they heard a terrible a sound that combines a cry and a roar, said the prince (Sands).):

- What does that sound creepy?

In her entirety, (Lilly), she turns to look at him:

- This is the bird people in captivity

- He said (in catfish style), looking at the horizon. :

- The sun is shining, people will open us with it

- Said the King (sage) seriously. :

Then let's use the stance for our need for this dense fog and shoot down once

Book of the damned episode 14 .. contact point last
Taking all fiercely fights
I did not recognize one of the tied horses, but the ease to the castle, and every now and then one drops a lifeless body on the floor without feeling the boy who was on guard, and it remains only a few seconds until I get (the kitten dies) to the square, who found him handcuffed to the railing, trying to break it and mix it, but she could not take it out quickly, another materialized, and suddenly the file (wise) and grabbed the sword with a strong blow, he violated all the restrictions, except for one of them, and now the bird took screaming and strongly Khader even noticed half a floor that seconds before they were in front of the king of charges they fiercely must take everyone who matches in ferocity

(Hot) I ran on the back of the bird people, which looks like an eagle, but the body of a lion and the rear tail of a bird, and the claws of an eagle, and the head of a predatory Eagle, and blows its wings into the air

One of the half-railers shouted a cry that he blamed his people for the bird that took to the air, still waiting for one of the restraints of his hind leg, but he continued to try to get rid of them.

Try to half the dog lure to the bottom of the memory of limitation, but it beats in the air harder, as if insisting on escaping from them, so the collapse of the limitation is strong, at the same time our heroes ran to the horses, and the half dog stubbornly pursued them into the forest.

While (the kitten dies.) Select the card in the sky ..

Then everyone heard the cry of a bird shaking around, and if you hear even half a word that they started to run, but they hid in vain, and suddenly appeared flying in the sky, but in a marvelous landscape risking all the laws of nature, where he caught his wings! and his tail was a fiery flame, flying behind him like something normal,

And they came to earth to burn everything, even the trees burned, opening their eyes in silence and surprise, not believing what is happening before their eyes!

Here she (Lily) said:

- Let's go catch up with him. they are interpreted in the way that trees in our country inspire fear of people.

And quickly flew (the kitten died) over the trees, moving which quickly moved to the road in front of her out of fear of birds; people on the horizon, the sun had already risen and the end of the forest and went to the top of the mountain, then she exclaimed (Lily):

- It looks like we finally got to the match

Without a word, they continued on their way, heading for the front.

* * *

What to do if the back of the mountain from afar until the person (tan) who turns forward scream

- It seems to be a popular destination, we (pigeon)

- It already exists.

- If you give us this damn book.

Note that the fish that received the cloudy black hosted a show of thunder and lightning from time to time, he accompanied us with the same, and the owner of the lightning and thunder said that she raised her eyebrows:

- (Burgundy) we need to go down, because it gets bad, suddenly it is possible that we will need it at any given moment, and let's continue our journey on foot

- As you can see, ignorance is not far off

Monday had already landed in front of a dense forest of trees, and behind them suddenly appeared our heroes, whose (burgundy) gaze did not certify and did not see, but (Lilia) stood uncertified and she also exclaimed stunned:

- (Burgundy) !!!!

- (Lily) !!!!!!

Everyone stopped and looked at them in surprise, and then quickly jumped on their horse and threw themselves on their knees to her brother, who held her tightly while she spoke, tears dripping from her eyes. :

- I thought I would never see you again

Look into her eyes and said:

- How do you know the way?

- It's a long story, I'll tell you today ... but I don't see my uncle Sheikh (Abdullah), where is he?

 His master's gaze into the ground understood this, and shouted:

- Remain God

She then went on to try to quickly change the subject, the situation needs no sadness now:

- We have already met a professional.

- Yes of course.

Book of the damned episode 14 .. contact point last
And finally, this is Burgundy's meeting with her sister Lilia
Then look at the queen (sage) and together with him briefly introduce him to them, then this is the role that we gave (to the dove) introduced him also briefly to them, and during this meeting the prince (Sands) unexpectedly shouted, which refers to sorrow

- What generation is this ruler?

Everyone looked to where he was singing (Burgundy) and was surprised to find that his eyes widened:

- What an amazing army I have never seen!

After (strands) with a sigh:

- I lost my book and ... ---

A certain King (sage) was associated with tourism, traits of persistence and sharpness of mind:

"They didn't put it down, and they won't leave it, it even glows from our hands.

There was a moment's silence, then his strong voice followed:

- Let's hurry to the other side of the mountain, let's go until the book is disposed of.

Indeed, turn everyone to the other side of the mountain, they will quickly rise, and at the top they have already left (A.J.) from the cave only to find the troops of the Queen of Darkness at the foot of the mountain screaming, shuddering with horror. :

- Oh my god, this must be a flood

It was the sound of drums shaking all over the front, but the owner did not set more time, but taking the ascent also to the crater of the mountain to get the book by Friday

And what if the queen of darkness to the foot of the mountain flew up through the air, climbing another mountain, and some people from the army followed her quickly, like a flock of fast rats, and in the background I saw the sky rumbling, and black clouds cover the sky , and the drums of war are beating hard, and far away the crows have begun to croak here and there

He was the first person who climbed to the crater of the mountain and shook him down (A.J.), and if he landed, he began to look for a book, and in this dim light he saw not far away, his jubilant heart danced and jogged to him and applied it to his chest, and what was happening around him was replaced with him, as with a living person. :

"Finally, dear, you deserve to end up between my arms.

And suddenly he looked like an angel, so I became like a madman, looked around and said:

- How do you run away now, and the dog is waiting outside?

Then he went on to say that his heart was beating wildly:

- How so? ... How so?

Take the one rolling without a gift, and quickly decided to climb the rope that fell on him again, and then climb quickly and suddenly heard a voice roaring frighteningly, coming from inside the cave, stopped using his eyes, the beats of his heart, but he decided to continue throwing off his current image again, and then the terror of its owner intensified, and quickly climbed up, and the dogs hung next to him.

The bellows increased even more and suddenly something grabbed the rope and jerked it strongly, as a result of which the Messenger of Allah (s) quickly fell after the director's proposal ..

Taking the drops to the bottom, he stretches out his hands, trying to hold on to the regiment, which took a smile upstairs, and this means dying of a broken heart, and if he fell on his back and sank to the floor of the cave, and his infa from the remote control, and pulled himself together, to catch something on his leg, past the eyes of its owner, and lowered his jaw to the bottom, and then pull that thing into the dark, letting go of him screaming with a great shaking heart.

Meanwhile, the queen of darkness entered the mouth of the well and landed, and I, hearing the cry of my mistress, tried to discern what was happening in the cave, but she could not hold the dark remote control in her hands, and he muttered these words. well then lit her scepter with a vision in front of her, there was a surprise waiting for her ..

Book of the damned episode 14 .. contact point last
He offered to take the book, and saw the giant beast.

He was caught in (AJ) a terrible creature human body, but with scales of green, sub-skin, his face, his ugly red eyes, sharp teeth and long claws

Khara's voice is annoying and he opens his mouth to the ground, oil drips from his lips, but the queen didn't give a damn about him when she saw the book, then quickly turned to her and took steps up from the crater of the mountain, and almost left until she attacked by this disgusting creature to quickly make her lose her scepter and associated stones, and then hard to fall to the ground ..

Trying to get up in search of the book, you lost him, but he again attacked them and stoned them hard in hot blood.

At the same time, both the king (wise) and his companions went downstairs to catch this scene in front of them, when a terrible conflict flared up on this creature up to the collar between our heroes and this monster, and when I felt that I was in the box, then quickly looked around.

Then he did something that no one expects. - - - was inclined to quickly hand the book to the one who fell on their ground and quickly catch it between his claws and show the file (wise) his target shouted to them strongly:

- Don't let him shave the worlds no matter what happens

It was already late, and a separate creature was lost, quickly spreading its wings, flying high along the nozzle of the cave, and behind it, which brought lightness and pleasure to the prince (Sands), and everyone climbed after him, later this creature was already flying

The prince came out (sands) and shouted:

- (Dove) my throat is behind this creature and where is he going?

Then I can quickly:

- The book is at his disposal

Book of the damned episode 14 .. contact point last
The strange creature's throat went up high and took out the book
A file (wise) came out, so that next to the prince (sands) and next to
him (Burgundy), and then after them (Lily) took aim at the next
creature, smiling and smiling, and behind him (dove) silently,

And below the army of darkness stood, flags fluttered on the masts
and drums beat, and here she, the Queen of Darkness, climbed out
of the well, hit her face hard and was torn in half. her clothes were
in a terrible state, but it was not really surprising, what is surprising
is the person helping her. he (Jafar)!

And what if you stood up and bowed in front of her, and there was
a belt from the bag and took out a mask, she was scary, the
butterfly moved terribly, creepy, dark colors, and then would give it
to her before she slowly and silently put it on face, and I took the
baton so that the horizon in silence was broadened by her eyes in a
strange way.

Rose shouted over the sounds of war drums as she took this
terrible creature, flew past a book about the sea and carrots and
cooked ..

And fly so far And ...

And disappeared over the horizon.

* * *

Returning (dove) and standing between the hands of our heroes to tell them about it

- I drowned the book in search.

The cry of the king (sage)

- How so?

- I dont know ! I suddenly dropped this creature into the sea and drowned, carrying the book to the depths, as if by magic or something invisible dropped it into the sea!

Here everyone started thinking, and you see who can fall on this creature so easily ?!

Almost everyone knew the answer.

* * *

In the middle of the sea was a hunter walking along his net for money, and it seems that with a valuable hunt, where is the weight of its weight, his heart elbowed, and I took it, wanting to be used, and did not know that there was a surprise waiting for him in his net ...

A surprise will change the fate of his life and many other people's fate

the end

www.ingramcontent.com/pod-product-compliance
Lightning Source LLC
Chambersburg PA
CBHW061512120726
48001CB00004B/1296